His touch felt way too good

"I'm okay now." Robyn didn't let go of his hand. She felt Ford slide across the big bench seat toward her. He slid one arm around her shoulders, and for a moment she thought he'd take her in his arms and kiss her. She kind of hoped he would.

She wanted his kiss more than oxygen.

It should have felt awkward as hell, but instead it felt like the exact right thing to do. She'd seen those old movie clichés of fireworks and waves crashing against rocks, but this was the first time she'd understood what those analogies meant.

Oh, God, he smelled good. The smell of his skin was intoxicating.

When his mouth finally made contact with hers, it was a sweet kiss, a gentle kiss, and Robyn didn't want it to end. She wished she could bottle the way she felt right now, all tingly and warm and strangely right with the world.

Ford slid across the seat, resuming his spot behind the wheel. "I've wanted to do that ever since high school."

Dear Reader,

Many years ago, I became fascinated by a news report about the Innocence Project, an organization dedicated to exonerating wrongly convicted people through the use of DNA testing. For years I've been mulling over the idea of creating a series of books about a similar organization. But the foundation I envisioned would use all sorts of methods for proving innocence—including a team of crack investigators, lawyers, evidence analysts and even computer hackers.

That's how my fictional Project Justice was born. For the record, Project Justice is inspired by, but not based on, the Innocence Project. I designed my foundation not as a factually accurate portrayal of such an organization, but to maximize dramatic possibilities, for this and future books.

Taken to the Edge involves a lying eyewitness, a sloppy police investigation and advanced scientific analysis of physical evidence—all of which have been used in real cases to overturn convictions. Of course, the most important aspects of my story are the human ones, the personalities, motivations and emotions of the people involved.

As of this writing, there are dozens of "innocence organizations" in this country and around the world, working to help those the justice system itself has wronged. I applaud their courageous efforts.

Sincerely,

Kara Lennox

Taken to the Edge
Kara Lennox

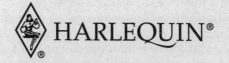

TORONTO • NEW YORK • LONDON
AMSTERDAM • PARIS • SYDNEY • HAMBURG
STOCKHOLM • ATHENS • TOKYO • MILAN • MADRID
PRAGUE • WARSAW • BUDAPEST • AUCKLAND

Recycling programs
for this product may
not exist in your area.

ISBN-13: 978-0-373-71689-0

TAKEN TO THE EDGE

Copyright © 2011 by Karen Leabo

ABOUT THE AUTHOR

Kara Lennox has earned her living at various times as an art director, typesetter, textbook editor and reporter. She's worked in a boutique, a health club and an ad agency. She's been an antiques dealer, an artist and even a blackjack dealer. But no work has ever made her happier than writing romance novels. She has written more than sixty books.

Kara is a recent transplant to Southern California. When not writing, she indulges in an ever-changing array of hobbies. Her latest passions are bird-watching, long-distance bicycling, vintage jewelry and, by necessity, do-it-yourself home renovation. She loves to hear from readers; you can find her at www.karalennox.com.

Books by Kara Lennox

HARLEQUIN AMERICAN ROMANCE

*Blond Justice
**Firehouse 59
†Second Sons

For my tireless editor, Johanna Raisanen,
who took the time and made the effort to figure out
where I belong in the large spectrum of
Harlequin Publishing. Johanna, your encouragement
and enthusiasm mean so much.

CHAPTER ONE

IF ONE WILD TURKEY ON ICE didn't make the pain go away, maybe two would. That was Ford Hyatt's thinking when he'd ordered a second drink even though he needed to drive home. But two didn't work, either, and now he'd have to sit in this damn ugly bar for at least two hours while he sobered up.

This never worked. He just wasn't a drown-your-sorrows kind of guy. He was more of a go-fix-what's-wrong kind of guy, except there was no way to fix this, no arguing with the fact that a woman was in intensive care, and it was Ford's fault.

His supposedly infallible instincts had failed him. Again.

"Another?" The bartender nodded toward Ford's empty glass.

"Sure." Hell, why not? In for a penny and all that. He could take a cab home.

He first became aware of the woman on the bar stool next to him when he smelled her perfume, a light, teasing scent. He looked over, surprised to find her there. She'd slid onto that stool as noiselessly as a cat.

"Need someone to drown your sorrows with?" she asked.

How had she known? Maybe it was just a lucky guess. Guy drinking alone in a bar must have some sorrows.

"I don't need company, thanks," he said. Or, more accurately, he doubted she would want his company inflicted on her. Under other circumstances, he might have responded to the flirtation. He gave her a second look from the corner of his eye. She was tall and long-legged, and dressed too nice for this dive. The fact she was hanging out alone at McGoo's meant he could probably have gotten her into bed without too much effort.

But the easy conquests of his youth held little appeal these days. Anyway, he was in a helluva mood. Being nice, even civil, would require too much effort.

She ordered her own drink, a diet cola, which made the bartender's grizzled eyebrows rise in surprise. Ford was amazed the bar stocked diet anything.

He gave the woman a third look—and realized he knew her. He hadn't seen her in well over a decade, and she'd changed quite a bit, filled out, darkened her hair a shade. But her eyes were the same, big and blue and innocent—deceptively so, some had said.

"Robyn?" He would probably regret starting a conversation. But he had to say something.

"I wondered if you'd recognize me. It's been a

long time." No smile, but why should there be? Their history wasn't exactly warm and fuzzy.

"You obviously recognized me," he said, wondering why she would even bother acknowledging him.

"I heard you hang out here sometimes. Your number's not in the book and no one would give it to me."

"Cops seldom list their numbers." God only knew how many wackos he'd arrested who'd love to find him, get a piece of him.

"Ex-cop now, isn't it?"

He nodded. "I left the Houston P.D. a couple of years ago."

"Why'd you leave?" The question sounded impulsive. "I mean, you were good at your job."

"Says who?"

"Well…everyone."

"You've been asking?"

"It's come up in conversation." She paused to take a sip of her drink, and Ford found his gaze drawn to her lips pursing around the straw.

Idiot. Yeah, so he'd found her hot in high school. The bad girl, forbidden fruit. Always in trouble. Not someone he would have gotten involved with. But that hadn't stopped him from getting a hard-on every time he saw her. Stupid how powerful adolescent memories were. He could suddenly remember every nuance of what it had been like for him back then, wanting something he knew would be bad for him, something that didn't fit in with his ironclad plans for the future. Doing the right thing, but wishing he didn't have to.

He took a gulp of his drink. "Any particular reason people have been talking about me?" he asked.

"Yes."

The single word hung in the air, and he knew for sure that this was no chance encounter, not just curiosity on her part. She'd come here looking for him, and she had an agenda.

"I assume you know about me, right?" she asked, her gaze not meeting his. "You heard what happened?"

Had anyone in Harris County missed hearing about the tragedy that had struck Robyn Jasperson's life? If they had, they'd been living under a rock. "Yes. I'm sorry." He didn't know what else to say. Stupid sentiment. Meaningless. But what could you say to a woman whose child had disappeared and was presumed dead? Nothing anyone said could make it better.

"Thank you." The rejoinder was automatic, probably uttered thousands of times since the tragedy—what, seven or eight years ago? At least they'd caught the bastard who did it…

That was when a disturbing possibility occurred to him. Oh, surely not. But the silence between them stretched uncomfortably.

He looked at her, and she met his probing gaze unflinchingly.

"Do you know why I wanted to speak to you?"

"I'm slow, but I'm starting to get an idea."

"You're not slow. In fact, most people agree that you are extraordinarily intelligent."

"You don't think Eldon did it?" he asked, incredulous. The D.A.'s case against Eldon Jasperson had been circumstantial, but it had been convincing— convincing enough for twelve jurors.

"No," Robyn said succinctly. "I do not believe my ex-husband murdered my son."

Without comment, Ford settled his bill and paid for Robyn's soft drink, too. "Let's walk outside." The stale-beer smell inside McGoo's suddenly turned his stomach. Maybe it was just that he didn't think someone as pretty and delicate looking as Robyn belonged in a place like this. McGoo's was close enough to the Houston shipping lanes that it attracted a rough clientele.

Outside, the air could hardly be called fresh. Summer in South Texas was never fresh, but the ninety-degree heat from earlier that afternoon had abated to a tolerable eighty or so, muggy as hell but not so bad that your clothes became drenched the moment you stepped outside.

A worn footpath ran alongside the twisty road where the bar was located. Without asking her permission, he led Robyn there. They could talk without being overheard. He realized too late she wasn't wearing good walking shoes, just some teeny blue sandals with her jeans and silk T-shirt, but she didn't complain.

"Why do you think that Eldon is innocent?" he asked point-blank. Project Justice, the charitable foundation he had worked for—until this afternoon—took on only cases with significant evidence to work with. The mere belief that someone was innocent, no matter how passionate, was not enough to get Project Justice to take on a case. There had to be new evidence, or perhaps a new way of scientifically testing old evidence, to meet the foundation's criteria.

"I have three things," Robyn said. Clearly she had prepared for this meeting. "First, a witness saw Eldon with Justin at the pizza parlor where he said Justin was taken from. Because the witness had drunk a beer—one beer—and hadn't gotten every detail exactly right, the police dismissed him as a crank and never even provided his name to the defense. But you, as a former cop, know that memory is imperfect at best."

"That's a good point," he said. "Any reason this witness wasn't mentioned during Eldon's appeals?"

"We've only just found him," Robyn said.

"We?" Ford's ears perked up. He wondered whom she was working with. "Are you teamed up with Eldon's lawyer?"

"Frankly, I have no money to pay a lawyer. 'We' is myself and Trina Jasperson."

"Trina—" It took a few moments for Ford to get it. "Eldon's current wife?"

"The one who broke up my marriage, yes." Robyn misstepped, and Ford grabbed her arm to keep her from falling.

"Maybe we should turn back," he said. "I didn't realize the footing was so bad on this path." The mosquitoes were out, too. He waved away a couple that buzzed around his face.

"It's okay. Let's keep going."

She probably wanted to prolong their meeting as long as possible to prevent him from walking away.

He took her arm again and firmly turned her around. "I won't be responsible for you breaking your ankle. Don't worry, I intend to hear you out. You've piqued my curiosity." Robyn and Trina, allies? Ford knew Trina Jasperson only by reputation, but that wasn't good. She'd been a party girl—possibly a call girl—before Eldon married her. "Frankly, I'm surprised Trina has stuck by him. She could have divorced him, gotten a huge settlement and moved on."

"Not all women who marry rich men do so for the money," Robyn said indignantly. "I didn't."

"Why *did* you marry Eldon?" Ford asked, then wished he hadn't. That hardly had any bearing on the case, and it was none of his business. But a detective never loses his strong sense of curiosity. Had she sought respectability? A stable environment to raise children? *Was* it just the money?

"Hard as it is to believe, I loved him. He saw things about me that others missed, saw good qualities in me that I didn't even know were there. He was good to me—well, to a point."

She sounded comfortable with that answer—as if she'd defended her position many times. "Sorry. That was a rude question for me to ask."

"I'll answer any question you ask—anything—if it'll help you free Eldon. He was hideously unfaithful, a serial cheater—that's one of the things the prosecution used to tear down his character. But he was a terrific father, utterly devoted to Justin, and I love him for that. He grieved for his son, all the while having to go through that investigation, incarceration, the trial. To the public he looked stoic, perhaps even cold, but I knew him in a way most didn't, and he was devastated by the loss of his son."

Ford knew that even murderers sometimes grieved for their victims. "Is that point number two?"

"I'm sorry?"

"You said you had three reasons you believed Eldon is innocent. The first was the witness at the pizza parlor. Is the second the fact that Eldon grieved for Justin?"

"Oh. No, I understood Project Justice wanted facts, evidence, not feelings. I was just answering your question."

"What are the other two points?"

Her heel caught on a rock and she stumbled again. This time she was the one who reached out for his arm to keep from falling. When she'd righted herself, she started to release him, but he grasped her hand

and wrapped it around his bare forearm. "Maybe you better hold on till we get back to the parking lot."

She didn't argue, and for the next couple of minutes, Ford found himself annoyed that he could not stop focusing on the feel of her warm, soft hand against his arm. How many times in high school had he vividly imagined sex with her? Yet he'd never thought about the experience of holding her hand, or listening to her talk, or the faint scent of that light, teasing perfume.

"The second point I would like to bring up is the wig fiber," she said, sounding more like an attorney than a…he didn't know what she was now, other than I rich man's ex-wife. "The cops combed Eldon's car bit by bit, and they found one lone fiber that didn't belong—a blond, synthetic wig fiber. They claimed it was insignificant, but I can't think of a single person Eldon or Justin came in contact with who wore a blond wig."

Ford loved fiber evidence. In years past, forensic scientists could declare one synthetic fiber "consistent with" another. But as testing became more sophisticated, precise matches were more commonplace, particularly with something like a wig fiber. That was something he could sink his teeth into. "I like it," he said. "But as I recall, the cops found blood evidence in Eldon's car, too."

"A few tiny drops. Justin frequently had nosebleeds."

"Okay. What's your third point?"

Robyn took a deep breath. "I believe Eldon was with someone that night, someone who could clear him. I know there's something he's holding back. There's a certain look he gets in his eyes when he's lying…about a woman."

Ford couldn't think what to reply to that. He had a healthy respect for a woman's instincts, but this was hardly hard evidence.

"I know what you're thinking," she rushed on to say. "But if I could just talk to him, I could convince him to come clean."

"You haven't talked to him?"

"They won't let me. And Trina—she knows nothing about the woman and I've hesitated to say anything to her. I don't want to be the one to tell her Eldon was cheating."

"I could probably get you an interview with Eldon," Ford found himself saying. The Project Justice lawyers were experts at negotiating prison regulations. "But why in hell didn't he speak up about this woman, if she exists?"

"He must have a reason. But I'm positive she exists." Robyn sounded like she was trying to keep the edge of desperation out of her voice.

"Maybe she's the one with the wig," Ford said.

"Exactly!" Right about then, Robyn realized she was still holding on to Ford's arm, and she pulled her hand back self-consciously. She wiped her damp palm on the leg of her jeans. "I'm sorry. I forgot I was holding on to you like that."

He hadn't forgotten. He still felt the ghost of her touch, like a brand on his forearm. "It's okay." He opened his mouth to tell her she could touch him any old time, then thought better of it. She'd come to him in a desperate frame of mind, and he would be lower than slime to take advantage of that.

"Robyn, it sounds like you've got some sound reasons for reopening the case. Have you talked to the original investigators? The District Attorney who tried the case?"

"Yes on both counts. They're like brick walls. Maybe you've never noticed this, but cops and D.A.'s don't like to admit they made a mistake. They particularly don't like to admit they sent an innocent man to death row. No matter what I hit them with, I get the same company line."

"'We're positive the right man is behind bars'?" He'd uttered that one once or twice himself when he was on the other side of the fence, and at the time he'd meant it.

"That's the one."

He'd once been that arrogant, believed himself infallible. He was a smart cop, everyone said so. Careful, conscientious. And still, he'd helped send an innocent man to prison—then, two years later, freed a guilty one.

He refused to make any more mistakes.

"I suggest you submit Eldon's case through the normal channels at Project Justice," Ford said. "I'll put in a good word for it."

"I've already done that."

Then why was she talking to him? Before he could voice the question, she answered it.

"The application process can take months. Do you know the date of Eldon's execution?"

It wasn't something Ford kept up with. "I'm afraid I don't."

"July 18. Exactly two weeks and one day from today. He's running out of time, and you're his only hope."

"Ah, hell." If Ford hadn't been sober before leaving the bar, he was now. He walked back toward his big Crown Victoria—the same type of car he'd driven as a cop, purchased at a police auction. Old habits die hard. "You're not making this easy, you know."

"I didn't intend to make it easy. An innocent man's life is at stake."

"Robyn, I no longer work for Project Justice."

Her eyes widened in shock. "What? Since when?"

"Since this afternoon. I quit. But I could try to get Eldon's case at the top of the pile—"

She shook her head. "I want you to handle it."

"I can't."

"Why not? I don't understand."

He wasn't going to explain it, either. But when he'd seen Katherine Hannigan lying in that hospital bed, literally black-and-blue, nearly murdered by a man Ford had helped to free, something had clicked inside his brain. He wasn't going to take people's lives into his hands anymore.

"I'll plead your case tomorrow morning, first thing," he said. "Give me your number. Someone will contact you within forty-eight hours."

"I want you to handle it."

In her chin-forward, clench-fisted stance, he caught a glimpse of that belligerent girl he'd known in school, the one who had so steadfastly maintained her innocence when she'd been accused of a theft.

The one he'd wanted to believe.

"Why me?" he wanted to know. "I thought you hated me."

She flashed him the ghost of a smile, then sobered. "My personal feelings for you are irrelevant. I know you're determined. I know when you get a case in your teeth, you don't let it go. And after years of being lied to by lawyers and scammed by private investigators, after having cops and D.A.s cover their butts rather than get at the truth, I want someone on my team who will work hard, stay the course. You're the ideal candidate."

Ford could hardly believe his ears. Why would Robyn Jasperson put so much faith in him? "How do you know that about me?"

"I pay attention."

They stared at each other, sizing up each other's resolve in the dimly lit parking lot as rowdy music from the bar's jukebox drifted out each time the front door opened.

"I've changed," he said softly, looking away.

"People don't change that much. Can you really walk away from a man who's going to die by lethal injection in little more than two weeks? If there's even a chance he's innocent?"

Damn it. He couldn't. He wasn't sure how she knew that about him, but she did.

"I'll think about it." He wouldn't make a promise he couldn't keep.

FORD DIDN'T TRUST MANY people, but Daniel Logan was someone he did.

Daniel had no training as either a lawyer or a cop. But six years in federal prison maneuvering through the ins and outs of his various appeals had provided him quite an education.

With the help of his billionaire father, Daniel eventually had found a way to prove he was innocent of his business partner's grisly murder.

Given his freedom and a full pardon, Daniel had wanted nothing more than to help others who didn't belong in jail. Thus Project Justice was born. His father had financed the foundation and Daniel ran it, though the employees rarely saw him.

"I never liked the looks of that Jasperson case," Daniel said after Ford had spent all day reading the trial transcript, then presenting his evidence to Daniel. They were in Daniel's study at his River Oaks mansion, which looked like NASA's ground control, given all the computers and research paraphernalia.

Daniel, tall and lean with a world-weary look that made him seem older than his thirty-six years, sat behind one of those computers rapidly tapping at the keys as he spoke. "The death of a child brings out the best and the worst in people. In this case, the people wanted blood. The cops and the D.A. gave it to them."

"The case was badly mishandled from the beginning." Ford sat in a leather wingback chair, Daniel's one concession to comfort in his high-tech lair. "A guy like Jasperson could have afforded the best lawyer in the country, and he chose some school buddy who couldn't tell his ear from a leaf of cabbage."

"Jasperson was an arrogant idiot. He wasn't worried enough to hire the best. He was so sure he would beat the charge—maybe because he was innocent. Maybe because he thought he was clever."

"I can't help thinking that if he were clever, he'd have done a better job staging a crime." Once Ford had started checking things out, he felt his blood thrumming. He loved the challenge of a complex case, ferreting out the tiny points of illogic, the inconsistencies everyone else overlooked.

"You know as well as I that intelligent people do stupid, stupid things, especially in the heat of the moment."

"So what's the bottom line?" Ford asked, intensely aware that the evening was slipping away. He wanted to have an answer for Robyn as soon as possible.

Daniel tapped a finger to his chin. "I think there's enough to warrant an investigation."

Yes! "I'd like Raleigh to take the case. She has experience with—"

"Raleigh just took on the Simonetti case, the guy who supposedly shot his girlfriend."

"Well, Joe Kinkaid, then. He's been asking for—"

"I gave him the Blanchard case this morning."

Damn. Who did that leave? Project Justice wasn't a large foundation. They received far more requests each month than they could take on, and regrettably had to turn down cases even when the evidence seemed strong.

"Who, then?"

"With your resignation—which I have not accepted, by the way—we're running at full capacity and then some. While I feel strongly that the Jasperson case should get some attention, I don't have anyone free. And I won't have any of my people neglect a case they've already committed to. Nothing gets done half-assed around Project Justice."

Ford knew that. No one got a job with the foundation unless they were willing to work nights and weekends when called for. Daniel was passionate about his vocation, and he demanded that same dedication from his people.

"The fact of the matter is," Daniel said, looking

up from the screen, "if you don't work this case, no one will." He sighed. "I simply don't have the manpower."

If it had been anyone else, Ford would have felt manipulated. However, Daniel Logan didn't play games, not with Ford anyway. If he said the personnel were stretched to the limit, then they were.

"Would you even want me to take this on?" Ford asked. "After the Copelson case…" He let that hang in the air.

"The Copelson case was a mistake," Daniel said.

"It was worse than a mistake. Using my skills to get that animal out of jail was a crime. They should have put *me* behind bars."

"Don't be melodramatic, Hyatt. The cops manufactured evidence on that case, and you proved it. He was unfairly convicted."

"Unfairly convicted, and guilty as hell," Ford muttered. He should have seen the guy's rotten soul oozing out his pores.

"Better to let a hundred guilty men go free than one innocent man—"

"I know the saying," Ford said impatiently. It was emblazoned on the gold seal in the front foyer of the Project Justice offices. He wished he could be as calm and businesslike as Daniel, to simply admit a mistake, learn from it and move on. But Daniel hadn't seen Katherine Hannigan in the hospital, the savageries done to her body. "So if I don't take the Jasperson case, no one will?"

"That's the truth, I'm afraid."

Damn it. "Fine," he gritted out. "I'll take it." But at what cost to his soul, he didn't know.

CHAPTER TWO

"Ms. JASPERSON!" CAME the panicked summons. "My pot keeps collapsing."

Suppressing a smile, Robyn hurried to the aid of one of her summer school ceramics students who was using a pottery wheel for the first time. Yesterday, his "pot" would have meant something else entirely. Today Arnie was lost in the throes of creativity, the feel of the wet clay, the joy of creating something out of nothing.

Sure enough, the tall, thin vessel he'd been painstakingly working on had fallen in on itself and was now a formless lump of clay.

"That's the fun thing about pottery," she said. "If you ruin something, you can just add some more water and start over. No need to throw it out. I think for this first pot you might try making something a little shorter and the walls a little thicker."

"But I was gonna make a vase," he objected. "For my mama."

"Vases come in all shapes and sizes." She loved it when the tough-talking kids expressed their love for their mamas. Arnie was still just a baby. He'd been arrested twice for defacing public property, but it wasn't too late for him to realize that creating something beautiful was a whole lot more fun than destroying something. She'd started this summer program after only a year of teaching. At first, she had donated her time. Now she received funding from a grant, enough to buy materials and pay herself a small stipend.

She showed Arnie an example of the kind of vase he might attempt. It was squat with thick walls, but it had a dramatic red glaze with blue streaks. "Can I make mine red like that?"

"Sure."

"All right, then." Satisfied, he followed Robyn's instructions for getting the new vase started, then she left him to his own devices and went to check her cell phone again. It was almost two o'clock, and she hadn't yet heard from Ford. His forty-eight hours would be up soon.

She didn't know what had disillusioned Ford. He'd been a serious student and athlete in school, a hard worker. But he'd also had an infectious smile—especially around people who needed cheering up.

He'd had no smile for her last night.

She knew she was right about him. He might have been wrong about her back in high school when he'd laid out her punishment for supposedly stealing those art supplies. But she'd recognized even then that he operated under a moral guidance system that saw no room for compromise. He'd seen things in black and white, right and wrong, just and unjust. And that was exactly the sort of person she needed to free Eldon.

"Okay, kids." She pulled herself back to the moment. "It's time to put away our supplies and clean up."

"What about my pot?" Arnie never took his eyes off the vessel he formed with clumsy hands.

Pleased that he hadn't given up at the first suggestion that freedom was imminent, she said, "You can finish up. I'll help you put things away."

A few minutes later, beaming over his crooked vase, Arnie flashed Robyn a grin. "Thanks, Mrs. J," he said as he washed his hands, speaking quietly so his friends wouldn't hear him being polite to a teacher. Then he grabbed his backpack and ran to catch up with the others.

Robyn's smile faded. Why didn't Ford call and tell her *something?*

A soft tap sounded on the door, and Robyn's throat constricted with apprehension. Could it be Ford? Had he come in person to deliver bad news? But Ford wouldn't be so tentative, she reasoned, and then she saw who it was.

She wasn't particularly anxious to see the woman who had replaced her in her ex-husband's eyes. Trina was everything Robyn was not—petite, curvaceous, exotic. She could also be a royal pain in the rear. But it was her husband in prison, Robyn reminded herself. It had been Trina's idea to contact Project Justice, and then to approach Ford personally, since he'd grown up in their town.

Robyn opened the door. "Hello, Trina."

Trina's eyes were shiny with imminent tears. "I couldn't wait to hear from you. I was going crazy just sitting at home and doing nothing."

Trina hovered at the doorway, peeking past Robyn into the classroom. She wore a short sundress that showed off her spectacular legs and matching sandals, her dark hair stylishly mussed, every eyelash in place. No matter what was going on in her life, she always managed to present a polished facade in public.

Robyn felt like a bum in comparison wearing her clay-stained jeans, her shoulder-length hair pulled back into a bandanna.

"Come on in. The kids are gone and I was just straightening up. I haven't heard anything yet."

Trina fairly vibrated with nervous energy as she click-clacked in on her heels.

"Why is it taking so long?" Trina said on a moan. She looked around, maybe for a place to sit, but in the end she just stood there. "Maybe we shouldn't have trusted Ford. Maybe he forgot about us and went golfing or something."

"He didn't forget." Of that Robyn was sure, though he probably wished he could. He sure hadn't looked happy two nights ago.

"Are you done for the day?" Trina fanned herself. The studio was always hot in the summer, both from the kilns and a lack of insulation against the blazing Texas sun. "I'll buy you a beer."

Robyn didn't really feel like having a beer at two in the afternoon. But Trina obviously needed companionship. "Where do you want to go?"

"Somewhere cheap," Trina said. "I have to watch my spending. The lawyers put a pretty good dent in our bank account, and obviously with Eldon in prison I have very little coming in."

Robyn tried to hide her surprise. Eldon had been worth millions. All of those appeals must have been costly, but could he and Trina have gone through that much money? Enough that Trina had to watch her pennies?

People had said Trina, a hairstylist, had married Eldon for his money. Eldon's high-society friends had never embraced her, and his parents had liked her even less than they'd liked Robyn. But Trina certainly hadn't balked at spending whatever was necessary to free her husband.

Since Robyn had been similarly judged, she tended to believe Trina really loved Eldon. The two women never would have been friends under normal circumstances, but they'd come to know each other during Eldon's ordeal, and Trina had been kind to Robyn when she'd grieved over the loss of her child.

Robyn never had been one to turn up her nose at friendship. Friends were in short supply right now. Many had deserted her after the divorce. Others had drifted away after the kidnapping, feeling uncomfortable around Robyn and her grief. The few close friends who remained thought she was insane for trying to free the man who killed her son.

Public sentiment against Eldon had been incredibly strong and still was.

As they reached Trina's white Cadillac, Robyn's cell phone rang. The ring-tone was an earthy hip-hop song one of her students had downloaded for her when she'd left her phone unguarded. Trina froze as Robyn fumbled for the phone.

"Yes?"

"It's Ford Hyatt. Can I meet with you and Trina?"

"Now?"

"As soon as possible. I'm at a bar and grill called Pacifica. Do you know where it is?"

"Yes. We can be there in half an hour."

"I'll be watching for you." He disconnected. A man of few words.

"Was it him?" Trina asked eagerly. "Is Project Justice taking on the case?"

"He wants to meet with us."

Trina clamped her eyes shut. "That sounds like bad news. He would just tell you over the phone if it was good news, right?"

"Let's not assume the worst," Robyn said, though she suspected Trina was right. Ford had sounded solemn. He might want to deliver bad news in person, to soften the blow. But then, Ford had turned into a solemn man. Again, she wondered what circumstances had caused that bleak look in his eye, and why she'd had to track him down at a bar where he was drinking—alone.

PACIFICA WASN'T THE SORT of place where Ford hung out. It was an upscale suburban bar, with a posh, funky decor that appealed to Houston's young professionals and where the martinis cost ten dollars and came in pretty colors.

Raleigh had chosen it. Raleigh Shinn was the senior attorney at Project Justice. She would consult on the Jasperson case, file the necessary papers and make court appearances. Ford liked working with Raleigh because she was thorough, knowledgeable and a hard worker. On the other hand, she was utterly humorless. He'd never seen her wear anything but a severe suit, her reddish hair slicked back into a tight bun. She had a pretty face and a stunning figure, but she downplayed her looks to a ridiculous degree.

As they sat at a corner table waiting for Robyn and Trina, Raleigh nursed a club soda.

"They're late," Raleigh said.

"Probably stuck in traffic."

"I've been digging around in the backgrounds of these two ladies. The first Mrs. Jasperson has a juvenile record, sealed. The second is no angel, either. She's been charged with everything from public intoxication to disturbing the peace to solicitation."

"Solicitation? I thought those were just rumors." What was it with rich men and their prostitutes?

"The charge didn't stick. I think she was more of

a party girl—sleeping with rich men in return for nice dinners out, clothes, jewelry. Eldon apparently had an appetite for bad girls."

"But by the time Robyn married him, she'd turned her life around." He'd done some digging around of his own. Robyn had gone to college and was now a teacher. Who would have guessed?

"Robyn, is it? First names?"

"She's an old friend. Well, acquaintance, anyway. I can tell you what's in her juvey record. Shoplifting, underage drinking, misdemeanor possession. But she went through one of those 'Scared Straight' programs and turned herself around."

Raleigh raised one skeptical eyebrow at Ford. "How do you know so much?"

"I went to high school with her," he admitted. "Green Prairie High was a good school, not too many troublemakers. Robyn was the exception." She had alternately fascinated him and horrified him. That a pretty, intelligent girl like Robyn would have such disregard for her future, that she would choose to hang around slackers, losers and dopers, confused the hell out of him.

He'd tried reaching out to her. He'd caught her alone for once, sitting in the cafeteria with a crummy school-lunch taco in one hand, the Cliff's Notes for *Hamlet* in the other. It was shortly after she'd returned from a stint in juvey.

He'd set his tray down across from her, then wished he'd rehearsed what he would say beforehand.

Normally he wasn't tongue-tied around girls. But Robyn, who seemed more adult and worldly to him than the other girls, had him flummoxed.

"You need any help with the Bard?" he'd asked.

She'd looked up at him, puzzled and not very friendly. "The what?"

"Shakespeare. The Bard."

"Oh. No, thanks, got it covered."

"I did *Hamlet* last year." Ford had taken all advanced placement classes, so he was ahead of Robyn, even though they were both seniors. "I'd be happy to help you study for the test."

She'd set her book down and stared at him. "Are you coming on to me?"

"I'm offering to help you study." And, yes, maybe secretly he'd been hoping something would happen. But he hadn't admitted that at the time, not even to himself.

She shook her head. "You have got to be kidding." She picked up her books and strolled away without a backward glance, leaving her half-finished taco behind.

Ford had mentally kicked himself for even trying with a girl like Robyn.

It wasn't long after that she'd been accused of stealing those art supplies and had come before the student government tribunal. She probably thought he'd voted her guilty to get back at her for rebuffing him. That hadn't been the case; he'd honestly thought her guilty and still did. But he'd taken some small gram of satisfaction from seeing her punished. In fact, he'd been the one to devise her penalty.

"Is that them?" Raleigh asked, nodding toward the door.

Ford waved to get their attention. "Yeah, that's them."

Curvaceous Trina Jasperson looked slick in a lime-green sundress, the neckline plunging to reveal impressive cleavage. Her hair moved just so as she walked her bouncy walk, and she wore enough makeup to lend truth to her questionable past.

Beside her, tall, long-legged Robyn wore a gauzy, paisley shirt and faded jeans with a big smudge on the thigh. Her hair was pulled back in a careless ponytail. No kitten heels tonight. She wore flat, leather sandals. And still, she made his mouth grow dry. There was something about her...she reminded him of a mustang filly, alert and high-spirited, loath to trust anyone.

He bet she'd hated coming to him for help. But she'd done it, to save the life of a man who'd cheated on her and betrayed her. That took guts, and he admired her for that.

The two women joined Ford and Raleigh at the table. By the time introductions were made, the waitress came by. "Can I get you ladies something to drink?"

"Bud Light," Trina said without hesitation.

"Iced tea, please." Robyn's polite smile faded the moment the waitress disappeared. She looked straight at Ford as if no one else were at the table. "Please don't leave us in suspense. Are you taking the case?"

"Yes. I'm sorry. I guess I should have told you that over the phone."

"Like, yeah," Trina said, grinning suddenly. "I was so nervous on the way over here I chewed the polish off my nails."

Rather than berate him, Robyn just looked relieved. "Tell us what our next step is."

Raleigh was prepared for that question. She pulled her briefcase onto the table and extracted a thick sheaf of papers Robyn and Trina would have to sign, basically naming Raleigh as the attorney of record for Eldon and holding Project Justice and its agents harmless, whatever the outcome of their effort to free Eldon Jasperson.

Trina peered suspiciously at her stack of papers. "This isn't gonna cost me anything, is it? I mean, like, y'all do this for free, don't you? Like a public service?"

Robyn visibly tensed while Raleigh, used to such questions, quietly explained to Trina the foundation would handle all reasonable expenses.

She worried at her lower lip. "My lawyer has told me not to sign anything without his okay."

"Jeez Louise, Trina, just sign the damn things," Robyn said. "We don't have time for more lawyers."

Trina looked chagrined. "You're right, of course. Do you have a pen?"

Ford fought the urge to reach over and touch Robyn's arm, to soothe her jangled nerves. They were all going to be pulling their hair out by the end of this thing. No use going into it frazzled. But he didn't dare touch her, not when he was so blatantly aware of her sexuality. He recalled her cold rebuff from high school and decided she might not welcome any friendly overtures from him, no matter how well-meant. She'd hired him to perform a service, nothing more, and he would do well to remember that.

With the legalities out of the way, Raleigh took off. She had a court appearance the following day, and her role on this case was strictly advisory. He would bother her only when he had legal questions or requirements—or enough evidence to move forward.

"She scares me." Trina took a long draw from her beer, which the waitress had just delivered. "I'm glad she's on our side. She should do something with her hair."

Robyn again tensed, her hands gripping her glass until her knuckles turned white.

"Raleigh is what I call coldly efficient," Ford said, attempting to ease the tension. "We're lucky she agreed to squeeze us into her schedule today. Are you ladies hungry? I can order up some food."

"I don't eat fish," Trina said. "They got something else here? Hamburger steak, maybe?"

"They have all kinds of things. I'll get you a menu. Robyn?"

"I'm not hungry."

"We'll be working a lot of long, stressful hours," Ford said. "I want you both to eat well and stay hydrated."

"You make it sound like we're running a marathon," Robyn said.

"We are, in a way. Given the deadline."

At this grim reminder, Robyn sobered and Trina's eyes filled with tears. "Try not to remind me, okay? I just get so upset every time I think about it." The waitress brought menus, but Trina waved hers away. "I can't eat, either."

With a sigh, Ford ordered himself an overpriced, rare tuna steak and a side of pasta. He tended to eat a lot when he was in the thick of a case.

Once the waitress left, Ford cleared his throat. "All right then, let's start at the beginning."

"What do you mean?" Trina asked.

"We can start with the weekend of the murder."

"Kidnapping," Robyn said in a firm voice. "Although realistically I know my son must be…gone, we shouldn't assume anything. All we know for sure is that he disappeared."

"Point taken. Eldon had visitation with your son that weekend?" Ford asked. He knew the answers to most of the questions he would ask, but he wanted to hear them from the source.

"Yes. He kept Justin every other weekend, and sometimes during the week, too. He seemed to enjoy the time he spent with Justin, never complained or tried to weasel out of it."

"He really did," Trina agreed. "That kid was everything to him."

"And was there anything unusual about this weekend? Any confusion or resentment, any arguments?"

"If you've read the trial transcript, you know that Eldon and I had an argument. But it wasn't a big deal like the prosecutors made it. His mother was trying to tell me how to raise my child, and Eldon thought his mother could do no wrong."

"You can say that again," Trina put in. "She's a control freak."

"It was just the usual stuff all divorced couples argue about. Not a big deal."

"So Eldon picked up Justin after work, took him to his house, and…where were you, Trina?"

"At a professional development conference. I was working to get my massage therapy license at the time."

"And this conference was…where?"

"Corpus Christi, at the Sheraton Hotel. I tried not to hang around too much when Eldon had Justin, so they could do their father-son thing without the evil stepmother getting in the way."

"The police verified your alibi?"

Trina nodded. "Oh, yes. A bunch of us from the salon where I used to work went to the conference together."

"Okay. So Eldon maintains that he was home, alone, with Justin on that Friday night. But for some reason he went out for pizza at midnight." Ford consulted his notes. "A large half pepperoni, half black olive pizza."

"Black olive?" Trina snorted. "Who told you that? Eldon *hates* black olives. I'm the one who likes olives."

"I got it straight from the police report," Ford said. That was when he realized Robyn was giving him urgent, covert hand signals to shut up—and he recalled that Trina knew nothing of the mystery woman Eldon had supposedly entertained that night.

Well, here was the evidence, pretty obvious even to someone who didn't know Eldon hated black olives. Most people don't order a half-and-half pizza for one person.

"That just goes to show you how incompetent the Green Prairie Police are," Trina said, all but spitting. "I mean, if they can't get a little thing like that right—" She stopped, thinking it through. Her eyes widened, and she set her beer bottle down with a clunk.

Ford looked at Robyn, not quite sure what she wanted him to say. Personally, he thought they should put all their cards on the table and work as a team. But he didn't want to be the one to spill it to Trina that her husband had cheated on her.

"He…might not have been alone," Robyn said gently.

"That's ridiculous!" Trina had turned pale under her tan. She scraped her chair back and stood abruptly, bumping the table and nearly upsetting their drinks. Several other patrons looked over to see what the commotion was about. "Eldon was not unfaithful! My husband loves me. He's always loved me. How could you say things like that about him when he's not here to defend himself? Hasn't he been bad-mouthed enough?"

"Trina…" Robyn tried, but Trina had turned and was already marching out the door, head held high, heels clacking noisily on the wood floor.

"Well, that went smoothly," Ford said, letting out a gusty breath.

"I told you Trina didn't know about the mystery woman," Robyn said.

"She would have found out sooner or later," Ford said.

"I didn't want to tell her unless we actually found the woman. Trina's been through so much—I didn't want her to suffer more."

"You've been through worse."

Robyn looked down, her lashes casting long shadows on her cheeks. "I won't argue that. But I've dealt with my grief. Trina's husband is on death row, and I can't imagine what horrible images haunt her at night when she's trying to sleep. I know she's kind of melodramatic, but she must be pretty torn up."

"Tell me more about her. Did she bear any animosity toward Justin?"

"Trina? No, I don't think so. I didn't have a lot of

contact with her until Eldon was arrested, but Eldon never mentioned any problem."

"Her alibi was solid? Corpus Christi isn't that far away."

"She had witnesses who say she was drinking in the bar until late, then she and her roommate went up to bed. She didn't leave the room until morning."

"That sounds pretty solid," Ford concluded. "What about your alibi?" He tossed the question out casually. He knew from reading the reports—and from chatting up Bryan Pizak, a Green Prairie cop he'd grown up with—that Robin had been considered a suspect.

Robyn shrugged. "I don't have one. I was at home, alone, sleeping like a baby while some animal preyed upon my child." She swallowed, and her eyes glinted cold and hard.

Ford steeled himself not to react to her emotionally. If there was one thing he'd learned in law enforcement, it was that emotions played no part. Emotions led you to form opinions, and opinions led to bias and tunnel vision. His goal was always to remain open-minded, unbiased, uninvolved. If that made him come off as cold and unfeeling, too bad.

She took a gulp of her tea. "The cops questioned me at length, of course."

"When something happens to a child, the parents are always the first suspects."

"Yes, they explained that. I guess I must have convinced them I had nothing to do with it, because after a few days they stopped badgering me."

"You think they focused in on Eldon pretty quickly?"

"Yes. Too quickly. They just didn't like his story, didn't like the way he was acting."

Ford couldn't help it. He flashed back to another time, early in his career, when he'd been called out to his first gang-related homicide. He'd been so eager to perform well, and he'd gone the extra mile, searching behind garages and around back porches in that seedy neighborhood, and he'd found a kid cowering in the bushes. Seventeen, wearing his colors, terrified.

Ford had made up his mind right there. He'd found the murderer. It was amazingly easy to do.

"People act all different ways when they become victims of crime," Ford said. "Some fall apart, some seem perfectly composed but they don't make sense, and some detach themselves from the crime completely and they come off as cold and uncaring."

"That was Eldon. He was not one to show his messy emotions in public. They said he was cold."

"It's enough to bias the investigating cops against him." Ford made a note to find those first cops on the scene and give them a good grilling. "Now then, what about this witness you mentioned?"

"He was an employee at the pizza place. Recently I talked with Mindy Hodges, who was night manager at the time. I've been tracking down witnesses one by one and speaking personally to them. She went over everything she could remember, and she mentioned an employee I never heard of—Roy. She doesn't remember his last name. She says he was there. He spoke to the cops, yet I never heard his name before now."

Ford made a note. Finding that witness would be first on his priority list.

They talked a long time. Hours. Ford persuaded Robyn to share his dinner, since there was plenty. By the time they were done, Ford had extracted every small memory Robyn had of the crime and the aftermath. He'd spent more time, focused exclusively on her, than he would have on a date. She'd been cautious at first, wary of saying something wrong. But gradually, as the hours passed, he wore down her caution and resistance until she quit censoring herself.

The challenging edge in her blue eyes softened.

Something else happened, though it was hardly unexpected. Ford found himself wanting her with the same intensity he'd felt in high school.

"Do you still smoke?" he asked abruptly, half hoping she would say yes. Nothing turned him off more than the smell of cigarettes on a woman.

"What?" She laughed. "Where did that come from?"

"I don't know. I just remembered that you smoked in high school. Down by the Art Building."

"How would you know what went on at the Art Building? You and your jock friends probably never set foot in there. Too afraid someone would think you were gay."

True enough. He wouldn't have been caught dead taking an art class. He'd taken music appreciation to satisfy his arts credits, and that was bad enough.

Ford shrugged. "I spied on you."

"You mean, you were like a student *narc?*" she said, her distaste evident.

He shook his head. "No, that wasn't it at all. I just liked to watch you." He couldn't believe he was telling her this. But the woman had just told him about her and Eldon's sexual habits, and he'd shared nothing with her. Not that working this case had anything to do with mutual sharing. But he appreciated her frankness, and wanted to keep the honest line of communication open. A little confession on his part was good for his soul.

"You were a Peeping Tom."

"I didn't say I spied on you in the girls' locker room." So much for confession. Maybe it was better if he abandoned this line of conversation. He could interrogate the hardest of criminals, but when it came to sharing his own feelings, he was a washout. Kathy, his ex-wife, had pointed that out to him with annoying frequency. When she wasn't badgering him to seek another promotion.

"I quit smoking when I got engaged to Eldon. He tried to make me over into someone worthy to be a Jasperson."

"How'd that work for him?"

"Not well enough, in his mother's opinion. She thought a degree in art was useless, a career as a teacher was common. And working with disadvantaged kids? Repulsive. 'God knows what sort of parasites and germs you bring home from work.'"

"I was blessed with a nice mother-in-law," Ford said. That had been one of the worst things about the divorce—losing Stella along with Kathy.

"Was? You're divorced?"

"I was something of a disappointment to my wife."

Robyn studied him, as if trying to figure out exactly what his ex-wife had found lacking in him. He didn't want to go there. It was a grocery list.

"It's late," he said, "and we have a long day tomorrow. Raleigh will get us the court order that will allow us access to all the evidence. When that happens, we'll get media attention, so be prepared."

"I hate reporters."

"Reporters are our friends. They're going to put the word out that we're looking for information and that we're willing to pay for it. Be nice to them."

"If I have to. What should I do?"

"You figure out how to get Eldon to admit he was with someone that night. We're going to visit him as soon as possible."

"What about Trina? She was pretty upset. Should I try to talk to her?"

"Frankly, I consider Trina a loose cannon. I sure

as hell don't want her talking to Eldon about his indiscretions before we can get to him."

Ford paid their check, refusing the money Robyn offered for her part. "I have an expense account."

As they exited into another warm, muggy night, Robyn stopped suddenly. "Hell, I don't have a way to get home. Trina was my ride."

"I'll take you."

ROBYN HAD TRIED TO DISSUADE Ford from taking her home. She could have called a cab. But Ford had insisted, though it was far out of his way to drive all the way to Green Prairie.

She was glad he drove a large car. Even so, it felt crowded. The big, muscular kid she remembered had grown into a wide-shouldered, slim-hipped man without any extra pounds anywhere.

Built for speed.

That thought gave her a pleasurable shiver. Not that she'd want him to hurry… Oh, God, why was she thinking along those lines?

Learning that he'd watched her in high school had unnerved her. She'd watched him, too, stripped down to gym shorts and a cropped T-shirt on the football practice field, all sweaty. She'd loved to watch him move. He had an easy grace that most kids his age had lacked, a comfort with his own body. He hadn't shown off and swaggered for the girls like some of his teammates, focusing on the drills with single-minded determination.

That was what she remembered most about Ford Hyatt—that concentration. If he took on a project, it got done. In the few classes they'd shared, he paid constant attention, took notes, asked questions. She remembered thinking how awesome it would be to have that attention focused on her.

Tonight she'd found out how it would feel. She should have been uncomfortable, pouring out the most intimate details of her life to him. Yet, after getting over her initial case of nerves, she'd felt okay talking to Ford. Good, even. It had been a relief to let down her guard and be perfectly honest—sort of the way she felt when she was throwing a pot or painting a picture.

She'd also felt more than one inappropriate shiver of desire. No man had ever *really* listened to her. Not the cops who'd interrogated her—they'd been more interested in putting words in her mouth and trying to catch her up. Certainly not Eldon, who wanted her to be the audience, soaking up his superior knowledge, following his instructions to better herself.

Being the sole focus of Ford's attention had made her feel like she'd never felt before. She'd had a hard time remembering that this was the guy who'd once judged her so unfairly.

Robyn still burned every time she thought of that high school incident. She'd been trying so hard—*so hard*—to be good for once in her life. A two-month stay in a juvenile detention center had been an eye-opening experience, enough to convince her she did not want to hang around those people anymore, ever. She'd made big plans to change, to make something of herself.

And no one had noticed. Not her mother, who was way too wrapped up in her own problems. Not her teachers, who'd already made up their minds about her. Not her old friends, who had barely noticed that she wasn't around anymore to smoke dope and spray-paint bridges.

But she kept on. And then came the unfair accusations, the humiliation of being accused of theft, the student government tribunal, which was run kind of like *The People's Court.* And Ford, head of the tribunal, student body president, so smug as he'd handed down the tribunal's decision.

She was kicked off the senior mural project. Looking back, it sounded silly that something so minor should still bother her. But her mural design had been chosen over a dozen others. It was the first time she'd excelled at anything, been chosen for anything, and she'd been as excited about it as a kid with her first finger paints. She'd been looking forward to having something positive to put on her college applications.

Ford had derailed all that.

She unearthed that old anger and held on tight to it as he drove her home. People like Ford could serve a purpose. That steel-spined sense of right and wrong, black and white and that dogged determination, were what she needed to free Eldon. But certainly no sane woman wanted a man like that in her personal life. No matter how good-looking he was. No matter how he made her stomach swoop.

Even if he was the first man to do so in years.

CHAPTER THREE

TWO DAYS LATER, ROBYN WAS getting antsy. After that first wave of urgency, Ford had become ominously silent. But when she got out of the shower that morning, the answering machine by her bed was flashing.

She pushed the button. "I have an appointment in Huntsville at two o'clock this afternoon," came Ford's no-nonsense voice. "I'll pick you up at eleven. Wear something conservative."

That was it. He didn't identify himself, didn't begin or end the message with pleasantries. Well, hell, it wasn't as if they were going on a date, was it? They were visiting her ex-husband in prison. Hardly a romantic outing.

Just the same, she dressed with care. She didn't have a lot of nice clothes. As an artist and art teacher, she tended to destroy clothes as fast as she could buy them, so jeans and T-shirts were the norm. But she did have a couple of outfits she'd worn to court. She chose her long, slim black skirt and a plain blue silk T-shirt, about as conservative as she could get.

In deference to the heat, she twisted her hair into a knot at the back of her head, holding it in place with a tortoiseshell comb. She refused to do stockings, but she wore high-heeled sandals.

She even wore makeup, something she didn't bother with most days. Halfway through her mascara, she wondered whom she was trying to impress. But Ford had told her to be prepared for the media, and that was what she told herself—that she wanted to look good on camera.

She was absolutely, positively not primping for Ford. That would be ludicrous and kind of sick, as well. She was trying to save a man's life.

Ford arrived promptly at eleven. Unfortunately, so did a TV van from Houston's Channel 6. It pulled right behind Ford's car, blocking him in.

Robyn *hated* reporters. She knew they weren't all scumbags, but the ones who lurked around corners and tailed unsuspecting crime victims rated no better than hyenas in her book. At the time of Eldon's trial, all they'd wanted from her was a sensational sound bite to crank up ratings.

Ford exited his car and faced the eager reporter and cameraman who'd leaped out of the van almost before it had stopped. Taking a deep breath, she grabbed her purse and went to join him. He'd said they needed publicity to shake information out of the bushes. But she knew from experience how damaging the wrong sort of publicity could be. If public sentiment got whipped up against Eldon, the governor was far less likely to stay the execution.

The reporters—more than one—spotted her the

moment she emerged from her upstairs apartment and were on her before she reached the bottom of the steps.

"Mrs. Jasperson, do you have any new leads as to the whereabouts of your son?"

"Has a body been found?"

"Why would you try to free your son's murderer?"

"Are you still in love with your ex-husband?"

She thought she'd been prepared, but the barrage of rapid-fire questions overloaded her brain. "I believe my ex-husband is innocent," she said. "As I have from the beginning."

"How do you feel about Eldon's current wife?"

"Do you know anything about Justin's murder?"

"Did you kidnap your son? Is that why you know Eldon is innocent?"

"Is your conscience bothering you?"

She wanted to tell them all what to do with their disgusting insinuations, but Ford had said not to antagonize the press. "I really don't have any more to add—"

"How do you explain Justin's blood found in Eldon's car?"

They moved in close, sticking microphones in her face, crowding her so that she could not escape. She'd never liked crowds, and panic rose in her throat.

Just then Ford pushed through the crowd and put a protective arm around Robyn's shoulders. "No more questions. We'll issue a statement soon, but right now we're on a tight schedule." He managed to sound cordial but firm, and the reporters immediately backed off. Ford escorted Robyn to his car, whispering in her ear, "You look like a scared rabbit. Straighten up and act serene and confident."

She tried. But all she could think about was reaching the haven of Ford's car and getting away from the insistent voices, wanting to rip her apart like carrion.

"Mr. Hyatt, aren't you afraid of putting another murderer back on the street?" one bold reporter asked after the others had fallen silent.

"If I were afraid I wouldn't pursue this case," Ford said with a tight smile.

He opened the passenger door and helped Robyn to climb in, acting the chivalrous gentleman for the press. Once the door was closed and locked, she took her first easy breath since Ford had arrived. She watched as Ford had words with a couple of men, and the van blocking their path moved out of the way as he joined her in the car.

"You okay?"

"Yeah." She took another cleansing breath. "You'd think I'd be used to it by now."

"You did fine." He started the engine, threw the car in gear and backed out all in one seamless motion. She liked the way he drove, all smooth confidence.

"Fine if you like scared rabbits." She still shook.

"Have you eaten today?"

"Yes." She'd had some toast for breakfast. "Is there some reason you're so fascinated by my diet?"

"You don't eat when you're under stress, and that's when you really should eat well."

How in the hell did he know that? But it was true. When she was worried about something, she either forgot to eat, or she nibbled because food didn't sit well in her nervous stomach.

"There's a white bag by your feet. I bought you a vanilla milk shake. Maybe not the healthiest thing in the world, but at least you won't pass out. Drink it."

She didn't like his imperious attitude. No one had ordered her around since she'd been in juvenile detention. Certainly not her mother, who had taken off with her third husband shortly after Robyn's high school graduation, apparently happy to be free of her daughter. But he was right; she did need something more in her stomach. She gave him a curt "thanks" and retrieved the milk shake from the bag. It was smooth and creamy and cool in her throat—exactly what she needed.

"What did that reporter mean?" she asked after a minute or so.

"Which one?"

"That last one, who asked you if you were afraid of letting *another* murderer back on the street."

"He was just trying to get a reaction out of me." But Ford's hands gripped the steering wheel more tightly.

"Have you ever made a mistake?"

"Who hasn't?" he tossed off.

"No, I mean, have you ever believed someone was innocent, and then you were wrong? Did you ever free a guilty man?"

There was a long, pregnant pause. "You must not read the papers."

"Not too often, no." Robyn sensed the tension rolling off him and debated whether to press him or let it ride.

"Drew Copelson. I got his conviction overturned. Two weeks after he got out of jail, he attacked and beat an elderly woman."

"Oh, my God. Did you—I mean, did you suspect—"

"No. I am, to this day, utterly convinced he did not commit the murder he was convicted of. He became a suspect because he had priors of violent crime, and he couldn't come up with an alibi. Forensics proved the police planted evidence to clinch their case. He didn't do it but I wish to God I'd left him in prison to rot. Katherine Hannigan wouldn't be lying in a hospital room right now."

"I didn't realize it was so recent," she said, wishing she hadn't brought up what was obviously a painful subject. "I'm sorry it turned out that way. But we can't just go around locking up people because they might commit a crime. You did the right thing."

"You wouldn't say that if you met Katherine. Or her family."

She hated the desolation she heard in his voice. She couldn't imagine what it must feel like to be blamed for the brutal attack of a woman. And clearly some people had blamed Ford.

"That's why I resigned from Project Justice. I was getting out of the guilt-and-innocence business. I would not be working this case if you hadn't pressured me." His hands gripped the steering wheel more tightly. "Clearly I should have gotten out a long time ago."

"I don't believe that's true. I've read about your other cases—the man in Atlanta who was accused of murdering his wife. The woman in Illinois who went to jail for supposedly killing her elderly father. I believe in our justice system, but it's only as good as the people involved. And when the system breaks down, someone needs to step in and fix it."

"I used to think that. Maybe I still do. But that person won't be me. Not after I finish this case." An SUV whipped in front of their car, cutting them off. Ford rammed his hand into the horn. "Damn, look at this traffic. Hey, have you talked to Trina?"

Robyn recognized a desperate ploy to change the subject. She let him. "I'm giving her a chance to cool down, but I'll check on her later. She's probably feeling betrayed by everyone right now, but once she thinks about it she'll see we're right."

"How did you two end up being friends, anyway?"

Robyn sucked up the last sip of her milk shake,

amazed she'd finished it. "I wouldn't exactly say we're friends. She did steal my husband, after all."

"In my experience, husbands don't get stolen unless they want to be stolen."

"Yeah, I know." She blotted her mouth with a paper napkin she'd found in the milk shake sack. "I was being flip. She's not someone I would choose as a friend. But when Eldon went to trial, his lawyer thought it would play well with the jury if both Mrs. Jaspersons presented a united front.

"Sitting next to Trina in the courtroom day after day, I got to know her. I'd always thought of her as the conniving 'other woman,' but I realized she truly did love Eldon. She's not a *bad* person. People condemn her because she was poor and married money, but they said the same thing about me."

"At least Eldon wasn't married when you met him. You were already making a better life, working your way through college, when you met Eldon. You weren't on the prowl for a rich husband."

How did Ford know so much about her and Trina?

"I didn't say I admired Trina. But I understand why she wanted Eldon. And I understand why he wanted her. Eldon has a pattern of taking on projects—young, unsophisticated, impoverished girls he could mold and improve. Once I was improved, at least enough that his mother quit badgering him to divorce me, he lost interest."

"Do you still love him?"

The question hung between them longer than it should have. Her answer should have been immediate—no. But she wanted to answer Ford just right.

"I'll always be grateful for the things Eldon did for me. He paid for my last two years of college. He encouraged me to get my teaching certificate. And he gave me Justin. Those two and a half years I spent as a mother were the best of my life.

"But I no longer love my ex-husband in a romantic way. He hurt me too deeply for that."

On that note, Ford ended his questions. He'd been nosy, and he'd gotten more than he bargained for—a glimpse of the raw pain Robyn had until now kept carefully hidden.

Not for the first time, he wondered if he was doing the right thing in pursuing Eldon Jasperson's freedom. He wouldn't take this case to the governor unless he was damn sure—a hundred percent sure—Jasperson was innocent. That was a pretty high standard. There was no way he would be responsible for putting another murderer—a child killer—out on the street.

If he bailed on the case, which was a definite possibility, he would dash Robyn's hopes and prove to her once again that she couldn't count on anyone. Getting involved in this was a mistake, but it was too late now to back out.

They arrived at Huntsville State Prison in plenty of time for the appointment Ford had arranged. Of course, they had to go through the usual security rigmarole. They were searched and scanned more thoroughly than a suspected terrorist at an airport, and then they were given a list of rules, verbally and in writing, detailing everything they couldn't do during the visit.

This was old hat to Ford. He'd visited more than one death row inmate since starting with Project Justice. But Robyn had probably not gone through this before. An inmate on death row was seldom allowed visitors, usually only with a compelling reason. Robyn was clearly nervous—she'd already chewed off her carefully applied lipstick and hadn't bothered to put on more.

When the guards were positive Ford and Robyn weren't packing a stun gun or bolt cutters, they were walked down one depressing corridor after another until they reached Cell Block H. There was no sign declaring it to be death row, but everyone knew what Cell Block H was.

They were shown to a room with a large table and four chairs bolted to the floor.

"Jasperson will be brought in shortly," one of the guards said.

When they were alone again, Robyn jumped out of her chair and paced. "I thought we would visit him through one of those windows with telephones—you know, kind of like in the movies."

"Are you nervous about seeing him face-to-face?"

She flashed a guilty, nervous smile. "Terrified. I

haven't seen him in years. Trina says he isn't holding up well."

"Sit down," Ford said. "You heard the rules. We have to stay in our chairs."

"Sorry." She slid back into her seat, then clenched her hands in front of her on the scarred metal table.

A few moments later, a guard escorted Eldon Jasperson into the room wearing shackles on both hands and feet, and Ford got his first good look at the man since the trial, when he was more familiar to Houstonians than the hottest Hollywood celebrity. Though Ford knew prison was hard on the inmates, he wasn't prepared to see a gaunt man with thinning gray hair and sallow skin. In the eight years of incarceration, he'd aged twenty.

The guard seated his prisoner in a chair across the table from them and chained him to it. Jasperson's gaze was on Robyn—and it was hungry. A surge of protectiveness welled up in Ford, so strong it stole the air out of his lungs.

"Robyn." Jasperson's voice was low, cultured. "This is a surprise."

"Hi, Eldon." She sounded soft, comforting, full of emotion. "I've brought someone to see you—someone who might be able to help."

Eldon spared a quick, dismissive glance for Ford. "Another lawyer?"

"I'm an investigator with Project Justice. Ford Hyatt." Ford nodded, since they weren't allowed to shake hands. "Are you familiar with Project Justice?"

Eldon's interest ratcheted up a notch. "You're the folks who get innocent people out of jail."

"Sometimes." Ford spent a couple of minutes telling him the basics of how the foundation worked and his role there. "Robyn brought your case to my attention. I'd heard of it, of course. But I hadn't realized how many unanswered questions remained. The information she provided was compelling enough for me to want to look into it."

"A little late, isn't it?"

"We're often the avenue of last resort. Mr. Jasperson, I'll get right to the point. I've read the police report, and I have strong reason to believe you were not alone the night Justin disappeared."

Fear and surprise flashed briefly in Eldon's sullen gray eyes, but he quickly hid his reaction. Not quickly enough, however. Ford knew he was on to something.

"Why would you think something like that? If anyone could back up my story, don't you think I'd have said something?"

"Why did you order a large, half-and-half pizza?" Ford asked.

He gave an exaggerated shrug. "Because I was hungry? Who the hell told you what kind of pizza I ordered? Why would anyone care about such a stupid detail?"

"It was in the police report," Ford replied. "Police

often ask for small details when they're questioning victims or witnesses—or potential suspects. The details will trip people up."

"Or help them out," Robyn said. "Eldon, you ordered a large pizza, half black olives. You *hate* black olives."

"That's just not true." But he swallowed several times. The questions were making him nervous.

Ford continued to push. "Mr. Jasperson, I can't imagine why you wouldn't tell us who you were with. Whatever your reasons for keeping that secret— surely they don't matter anymore. You have nothing to lose."

"I'd like to help, believe me," Jasperson said politely. "But I was alone."

Robyn banged one fist on the metal table. "You were cheating on Trina while she was away at a conference," she said, suddenly harsh. "Why can't you admit that?"

"Where would you get such a foolish idea?" Jasperson sounded less polite now.

"Because you cheated on me. And I know what it looks like. I watched the video of your interrogation, and I know the look that was on your face. I've seen it before—when you'd been with Trina and you were trying to hide it from me."

He sat up straighter, defiant. "Maybe I looked guilty on that video because I killed our son."

Ford expected Robyn to flinch at the words, but

she came right back at him. "I know damn well you would never have hurt Justin. Tell me who she is."

Robyn and her ex-husband stared at each other, challenging, until Ford was sure blue sparks would fly between them. But finally Eldon looked away, defeated. "I can't find her," he said softly. "I saw no reason to involve her at the beginning. I had no clue things would turn out as they did, not an inkling that I'd be arrested for Justin's murder. So I said I was alone. Later, when I knew I was in trouble, I couldn't find her. She'd left town. So I said nothing. Changing my story—with no one to corroborate it—would only make me look like a liar. And a cheating husband on top of that."

Ford resisted the urge to grin. He really hadn't been sure Robyn's hunch would pan out.

"So what's her name?" Ford asked, pad and pencil ready.

Eldon shook his head. "You won't find her. She hid her tracks well. Anyway, she wasn't there when Justin was taken. She was back at my house."

"But she can verify that Justin was alive at the time you left to get pizza." Ford was amazed that Jasperson didn't grasp this. "The prosecution has always maintained the pizza run was a cover story used to stage a phony kidnapping, and that you'd probably killed Justin hours earlier and spent a good amount of time disposing of the body."

Now both Robyn and Eldon *did* flinch.

"I'm sorry, but there's no time to worry about

delicate sensibilities. Eldon, this woman could clear you."

"I doubt she'll talk, even if you do find her."

"Let me worry about that. What's her name?"

"You can't do this!" Eldon roared. "Trina...Trina has been so loyal through all this. I can't face death knowing I've turned her against me."

"Eldon," Robyn said. "It's too late for that. She already knows."

"She's okay with it," Ford added, lying through his teeth. "She understands. She won't hold it against you, not at this late date. It was a long time ago."

Eldon shook his head stubbornly.

"You'd rather die than take this chance?" Ford asked.

He didn't respond.

"We'll find her without your cooperation," Ford said with steely determination. "And when we do, I won't be gentle with her. I'll feed her name to every sleazy reporter in the country. Her life will be a living hell."

ROBYN WANTED TO OBJECT to Ford's harsh threat. Hadn't Eldon been savaged enough? But what did Ford care? He didn't know Eldon, had never seen him playing horsey with Justin or entertaining the baby with faces while changing his diaper. Ford's job wasn't to make friends. He was pursuing this case the way he did everything—moving resolutely forward, eye on the goal, never wavering.

It was the reason she'd agreed with Trina that he was the right man for the case.

When Ford had shielded her from the media vultures, she had thought she'd seen a speck of caring there. But she must have been mistaken. The man was a machine.

"Eldon," Robyn said gently, grasping his attention. "No matter what happens, you won't die alone. I will be here for you. I still care for you."

"How could you?" he asked. "After what you've been through…"

"You lost a son, too. Maybe you aren't the most faithful of husbands, but that doesn't mean you didn't love your son—or that you should die for someone else's crime. For the love we had for Justin—for the love we once shared. Help us help you." A single tear escaped, and she dashed it away. "Tell us the woman's name. We'll handle it sensitively."

Eldon closed his eyes, battling some internal demon. Finally he looked at Robyn, shutting out Ford. "Heather." He barely whispered the word. "It was Heather."

"Heather Boone?" Robyn asked, her voice coming out a hoarse accusation. Oh, God. No wonder he hadn't wanted to say anything.

"Do you understand now?"

Robyn was afraid she did. "How old was she at the time?" She chanced a look at Ford, gauging his reaction. He leaned back in his chair, his face a granite wall. But she noted a faint flicker of displeasure in his eyes. He wasn't happy with the conversation's direction.

"She was above the age of consent," Eldon said.

Ford suddenly sat forward. "Look, would somebody mind telling me who Heather Boone is?"

"She was one of my art students. Someone I took a special interest in. Apparently Eldon did, too," she added bitterly. "Damn it, Eldon, she was a troubled child. How could you take advantage—"

"I was helping her."

"By sleeping with her?"

"Time-*out!*" Ford silenced them with his outburst. Robyn looked at him, startled at his show of temper. But there was a time to be sensitive, and a time to play hardball. Ford instinctively knew which strategy to use. "If you want me to move forward with this case, y'all are both gonna have to shut up and listen to me. Eldon, you're dealing with me now, not your ex-wife. Tell me from start to finish what happened that night. And if I sense any bullshit, I'm walking out of here and never coming back."

CHAPTER FOUR

ROBYN SHRANK BACK IN THE face of Ford's anger. She wasn't used to people speaking to her that way. Most people, family included, handled her with kid gloves. They tolerated any sort of emotional outburst or bad behavior because she had lost her child to tragedy.

She stared at Ford and he at her, bracing for more harsh words. But they didn't come. After a few charged moments he sat back in his chair and straightened some papers on the table in front of him.

Robyn switched her attention to Eldon, positive he would be the next to explode. Her ex had never tolerated anyone speaking to him in such a manner—which hadn't boded well for him during police interrogations. But to her surprise, he didn't strike back. He folded his arms and looked down in a classic posture of submission.

He hardly looked like the man she knew. Or thought she knew. God, he'd had an affair with a teenager. A girl still in high school. Barely legal. Of course, Robyn had been the same age when Eldon had first become interested in her; Trina had barely been out of her teens at the time Robyn discovered that affair.

"I'll go over the story again," Eldon said calmly, as if the outburst hadn't happened. "If you think it will help."

He started at the beginning, when he had picked up Justin from Robyn's house and they'd argued about his mother's interference. His story lined up with her own—possibly because they had both told it so many times that their memories had become identical.

When he got to the part about Heather, he spoke barely above a whisper, so that Ford had to ask him to speak up so the digital recorder could pick up his voice.

They had spent the evening as people having illicit affairs generally did. Then Heather, with a case of the postcoital munchies, had begged Eldon to order pizza. He'd gone to pick it up, he said, because the restaurant didn't deliver past midnight.

"Why did you take Justin with you?" Ford asked. "Why didn't you leave him at the house if Heather was there?"

"He woke up just as I was about to leave, crying and cranky. Heather didn't know anything about taking care of children, and she wasn't comfortable alone with him. I scooped him up and brought him along because he liked to ride in the car. It usually put him right to sleep, which I thought would be a good thing."

"And did he fall asleep?" Ford asked, scribbling notes.

"The restaurant was less than ten minutes away. By the time I got there, Justin was out like a light. That was why I left him in the car. I didn't want to wake him up. I know it was wrong—crazy wrong—but the pizza place was in a nice neighborhood. The parking lot was well lit. I was going to run in, grab the pizza and run back. I was gone less than two minutes."

"And when you came back?"

He shook his head. "I almost didn't notice he was gone, at first. The car was dark, and I was anxious to get back home. I turned around to back out and… that's when I noticed."

"What did you do?"

"For a minute, I just stared in shock. Your mind goes through all the usual stuff—maybe I was seeing things. Maybe he got out of the seat and moved to a different part of the car. Maybe he wandered off. He'd just recently learned to get himself out of that car seat.

"Or maybe I hadn't brought him with me—maybe he was at home. I considered everything, including that I might be going crazy. Then I started searching. And calling. I had every employee from the restaurant searching inside and out. And when he didn't turn up after a few minutes, I called the police."

Despite everything, Robyn's heart went out to him. She could see the torture on his face. His lawyer had elected not to put him on the stand during his trial, claiming that it was always a risky move. The D.A. could trip up even the most innocent defendant.

Now she believed it had been a mistake not to let the jury see Eldon's raw pain. He hadn't shown this side of himself to the media, but if they saw him now, they would never refer to him as cold again.

She couldn't even imagine the guilt he must feel. If she'd been in his shoes…well, she never would have left Justin in a car unattended, under any circumstances. But children were snatched from even the most attentive parents.

Robyn thought the interview was over. Eldon had finished his story. But Ford had more questions.

"What happened to Heather?" he asked. "When you didn't come home with the pizza—did she call you? Did she come looking for you?"

"No. I was so focused on finding Justin, I completely forgot about her. And when I came home—hours later—she was gone. She'd left an angry note, which I destroyed."

"Did it surprise you that she didn't call?"

Eldon hesitated. "She was…melodramatic. She probably assumed I was with another woman. Such a reaction is not completely normal, I know, but it's what she likely would have done."

Ford looked to Robyn for confirmation. She nodded. The Heather she had known was borderline paranoid. Everything was about her. In her mind, people and events all conspired against her.

"Did you continue your affair with her?"

"God, no. I was living in a fishbowl after Justin disappeared. By the time I realized I was a suspect, Heather had left town. I didn't see the point in dragging her into it—tearing up my marriage and my character in the process—if she couldn't be found to back me up."

Robyn watched Ford. His face gave away little, but she sensed a prickle of excitement coming to life inside him. They'd barely started, and already they had a new lead.

Still, the questions continued. They talked almost three hours, until a warden told them they had overstayed their welcome.

As they took their leave, Robyn searched for something to say to Eldon. Something to ease his pain, to reassure him, to give him a thin shred of hope to cling to.

But she could see nothing they'd done here today gave him hope. He was a defeated, broken man.

"Eldon," she said. It was the first she'd spoken since her outburst. "You're not alone. I won't abandon you, and neither will Trina. She loves you."

Eldon shook his head. "You both loved a man who didn't really exist." On that note, a guard escorted him away.

Robyn didn't take a good, deep breath until they were outside. She had never appreciated hot, muggy, *fresh* air so much in her life.

"It must be awful for him," she said as they walked

across the steaming parking lot toward the car. "Eight years behind bars, most of them in that place."

"It's bad," Ford agreed. "Guilty or innocent, it changes a person forever." He opened the passenger door of the Crown Vic. "Robyn, what do you think he meant when he said you loved someone who didn't exist?"

She leaned her back against the car. "I guess because we both thought he was a devoted husband. When in reality he was jumping everything in his path with an X chromosome."

"There were others?"

Robyn slid into the passenger seat and waited until Ford was behind the wheel. "Trina was the third one I knew about. When I caught him with the first one, he swore it had been a onetime deal, a momentary lapse, and that it would never happen again. I was pregnant with Justin at the time, and I didn't want to make waves, so I chose to believe him.

"After the second one, I threatened to leave, but he said he would get counseling, and he did. The salon where Trina worked as a shampoo girl was next door to the counselor's office."

"What a bastard," Ford muttered.

"I know you must think I'm an idiot."

"Not at all. Eldon's a good liar, very convincing. He turns those emotions on and off like a faucet."

Robyn sat up straighter. "You think he was lying?" she asked, alarmed. If Ford believed Eldon was guilty, he would drop this case so fast her head would spin.

"No. The story he told today sounded legit. I tried every which way to trip him up and I couldn't. But he was faking some of that angst. Milking his anguish and regret for all it was worth. For your benefit."

"Mine?"

"You're his last ally. He might lose Trina and he knows it. He's going to manipulate your emotions every which way to make sure you give this your all. He's a master manipulator, Robyn. I've been dealing with his type my whole life."

Robyn squeezed her eyes shut. "You're going to drop the case."

"What? No. I told you, I believe his story. The guy doesn't deserve the needle for being a cheater. I just want you to promise me one thing."

"What?" she asked warily.

"If we get Eldon out of jail, you'll have nothing to do with him. Ever."

"But if he gets out, he'll need—"

"Ever. Promise me, Robyn."

Why did Ford care? "I could promise anything. How do you even know I would keep my word? I'm a liar, remember? I lied about stealing those art supplies."

Oh, hell, why had she brought that up again? It was so many years ago, and revisiting that time only served to put her and Ford against each other. But the memory had never completely lost its kick. Whether falsely accused of a murder or a minor theft, it felt awful.

"So you admit you were lying?" His tone was conversational, curious.

"Of course not. I didn't steal the damn art supplies."

"Look, whatever I believed about you then is immaterial. If you make me a promise today, I'll trust you."

"I promise I won't ever become involved, romantically, with Eldon Jasperson. But if he should be freed from prison, I wouldn't turn my back on him. I told him he wasn't alone, and I meant it. Deal with it."

"In high school, you never would have stuck your neck out for someone else."

"You think you knew me in high school. Had me all figured out, huh? After one conversation?" Her face heated as she remembered how rudely she'd rebuffed him. But what had he expected? She'd had no reason to trust him or his motives.

"I knew more about you than you might guess." Ford actually smiled. His gaze was faraway, but something about the past tickled him. It was the first time she'd seen him even crack a smile since she'd walked up to him at that seedy bar. The brief show of humor lit up his face and changed his whole countenance.

"What?"

"Just that I had a crush on you as big as a football field."

"No way."

He quickly sobered. "I don't blame you for doubt-ing me. But why else do you think I came up to you in the cafeteria?"

"How should I know? Maybe it was a bet. Or…or you wanted to make fun of me somehow. Everyone else did. I made an A or two, turned in a few home-work assignments, and people looked at me like I'd grown horns and a tail."

"That's not how I looked at you." His voice had gone rough, and Robyn's skin prickled as a tiny kernel deep inside her grew hot.

His meaning was clear. He'd wanted her. Her body was reacting to a boy's passing fancy he felt twelve years ago. Ridiculous. Nothing could have possibly happened between them then, and it sure as hell couldn't now.

To this day, Ford thought she'd stolen a closetful of art supplies. Despite the fact she'd lived an exemplary life. She was done allowing anyone to judge her in any way, especially an ex-cop who apparently judged himself the most harshly.

"I'VE GOT SOME GOOD NEWS for you," Beth McClel-land, Project Justice's forensics expert, told Ford. Another refugee from the Houston P.D., recruited by Ford himself, Beth coordinated the analysis of physical evidence. She could do some things in Proj-ect Justice's own small lab. But for more specialized work, Beth had at her disposal a slew of experts all over the country who did everything from paint and glass analysis to blood spatter. And they did it in a hurry.

Ford looked up from his computer screen and rubbed his eyes. "I could use some good news."

His attempts to locate the mysterious witness, "Roy," had met with utter defeat. The pizza restaurant had gone out of business, the former owner had disappeared, the other employees were flung far and wide.

So he'd focused on Heather Boone, trying to find someone who had an idea of her whereabouts. She had no family left in Green Prairie. She wasn't "missing," in the sense that no one had reported her to the police. She had simply vanished.

It had been three days since he and Robyn had been to the prison, and he hadn't made much progress in the investigation. His discussion with the District Attorney who had prosecuted Eldon had been like talking to a brick wall.

He'd had better luck with the Green Prairie police. His high school buddy Bryan Pizak had again been helpful. When Ford had shown up with the court order, Pizak had quickly and willingly supplied a copy of the case file and the boxes of evidence.

Ford had expected to find cartons and cartons of evidence. A high-profile case like that, usually police went overboard collecting everything.

He'd been surprised when the clerk at the warehouse where they kept old evidence had brought him only two cardboard boxes. In them, he'd found very little of use—except for that lone wig fiber Robyn had mentioned.

He'd turned the fiber over to Beth, carefully maintaining a chain of evidence, and he guessed her news was related to that.

Beth settled into a wingback chair across from Ford's desk, looking more like a secretary with a juicy piece of gossip than a hard-nosed scientist. In her late thirties, she had a headful of chocolate brown corkscrew curls and big, innocent blue eyes. Though she claimed to be a "science nerd," she always appeared stylish, favoring bright colors and bold jewelry.

She never wore a lab coat unless she was actually in the laboratory with her test tubes and chemicals.

"So, what do you have for me?"

"You're lucky. That wig fiber is quite unusual, at least around here. It's manufactured in Germany, and there's only one brand of wig sold in this country that uses it. It's made by a company called Brandenburg. Their highest-end wigs are in the Allure line. The color is wheat."

Once again, Ford was amazed at the speed with which Beth came up with her detailed information. "How did you learn all that?"

"I just analyzed the fiber, but I know a guy in Oklahoma who has a huge database of fiber compositions for anything synthetic. Wigs, carpet, any kind of fabric."

"You have once again earned your keep."

"Tell Daniel to give me a raise."

Ford knew she was kidding. Daniel paid her and everyone else on his staff far more than they could earn in the public sector, let alone if they got a corporate job. He only hired the best and he did his best to keep them.

"There's more. The Allure line was only manufactured for a couple of years, right around the time of the murder. I emailed you a report."

Ford still didn't have a lot of hope he could track down the wig or who was wearing it. But he had to follow every lead, and this was one he could turn over to his helpers. Robyn had been itching to make herself useful. Calling every place that sold wigs in the greater Houston area wasn't glamorous, but it didn't require much skill, either. He would rather save Project Justice's skilled investigators for more challenging tasks.

"Thanks, Beth."

She smiled, and reached across the desk to squeeze his hand. "My pleasure. And, for the record, I'm glad you changed your mind about leaving."

"I didn't. When I'm done with this case—"

"It wasn't your fault!"

Any number of people had told him that. But plenty had told him just the opposite. Katherine Hannigan didn't blame him, but her family sure did.

Ford didn't want to argue with Beth. "Thank you,"

he mumbled, then pointedly returned his attention to his computer screen.

And suddenly, there she was. Heather Boone. One of her old classmates had responded to an email Ford had sent, requesting any information. Heather was now Heather Brinks, married to a minister and living in Ardmore, Louisiana.

A few more clicks on the computer, and he had her address.

He picked up the phone and dialed Robyn's cell number. She had made herself available to him 24/7, assuring him he could call anytime he needed her help, and she would drop what she was doing.

As it rang, he was amazed at the anticipation he felt waiting to hear her voice. He'd spent at least as much time thinking about Robyn as he had about the case. She was even more attractive now than in high school, and she'd been a schoolboy's fantasy back then.

Maturity had softened her. She'd put on a few sorely needed pounds in the past twelve years, though she was still slender as a blade of grass. Her face was softer, too. But he could still drown in those huge blue eyes, and he could still imagine kissing those full lips.

Not that it would ever happen. He felt a certain chemistry with her, but whenever she remembered their thorny history, she looked at him like he was something she'd scraped off her shoe. Sadly, there was no way to change that. She couldn't undo the fact that she'd been a juvenile delinquent, and he couldn't undo the fact that he'd judged her.

He knew she'd turned her life around. He might be able to dismiss her past, but she obviously couldn't put it behind them. He was serving a purpose in her life right now, nothing more.

ROBYN SET THE LAST POT into the kiln and closed it.

"So is this like my oven at home?" Arnie had been hovering at her elbow, watching her every move. Earlier, he had applied glaze to his squat vase with an intensity born of passion. The other kids in the class—she had twelve in all—had seemed to enjoy the process. Some had globbed on every color they could get their hands on, others had inscribed names or words or even gang symbols into their pots.

Some had taken their time and some had just gotten it over with as quickly as possible so they could mess around. Robyn didn't hammer on discipline too much, since this was supposed to be a fun class even if they did get school credit.

Arnie, however, had approached his vase with the sober intensity of a budding artist. He had a good eye but, having never picked up a pencil or paintbrush, he lacked skills. Robyn could provide him with those skills, and he absorbed techniques as fast as she could teach them. She was watching his artistic talent come alive before her eyes, and it was one of the most rewarding experiences of her career.

"Unfortunately," she said, "you can't fire this kind of pot in your oven at home. It doesn't get hot enough. This oven gets up to eighteen hundred degrees."

"Damn."

"But they do make clay you can fire in a regular oven. It comes in different colors. Rather than glazing it, you combine the colors in an interesting way."

"You got any of this clay?"

"Not here. It's kind of pricey."

"How pricey?" he asked warily.

"I'll find out. Maybe I can get the craft store to donate some for the class."

"But I want to do this at home. The art class is gonna be over in a couple of weeks. And those wheels—how much do those cost?"

Robyn smiled. She'd created a monster. "Pottery wheels are quite expensive. But I found my wheel at a garage sale. If you keep your eyes open, you might be able to find a good used one for—" she winced slightly as she said it "—two hundred dollars."

Arnie deflated. "I ain't got two hundred dollars. I ain't got twenty dollars."

That was probably a good thing. Although he'd never been charged, the police suspected Arnie had been dealing drugs. If he was broke, it probably meant he was keeping his nose clean.

"Arnie, I promise you. If you really want to make more pots, I'll find a way to make it happen." Even if she had to give up her free time to hang out here so he could use the school facilities. She would pay for the materials out of her own pocket if she had to.

"That's cool." He pointed to the kiln. "How long before these pots are baked?"

"Fired. Not until tomorrow."

"Oh. Can I come see tomorrow?"

"I'll have them all ready for class on Thursday. For the next few weeks I'm going to be pretty busy, but then we'll talk about getting you some more hours in the studio, okay?"

"Cool." He didn't seem to be worried today that his friends would see him sucking up to the teacher. He was riding an artistic high. She knew how that felt. She remembered her first pot. It now sat on her kitchen windowsill, growing oregano. It was far uglier than Arnie's would turn out.

Robyn felt a prickling at the nape of her neck. She looked toward the door and took a sharp breath. Ford was standing there, watching her through the window.

How long had he been there?

She couldn't wait to hear his news. He wouldn't tell her on the phone. All she knew was that he wanted her to go with him on a long drive someplace.

Thank God she'd brought a change of clothes with her today. She was covered with clay and glaze and coffee she'd spilled in her car this morning.

She waved to Ford, letting him know she'd seen him.

"Has everybody cleaned their brushes and put them away?" she asked the kids. "Britney, is that your mess on that table? Kelly, will you put those jars of glaze back in the cabinet, please?"

They all knew she wouldn't let them leave until the room was put back in order, so they didn't argue.

She walked to the door and opened it. God, he looked good. He had on a crisp linen shirt, black jeans and black cowboy boots. For some reason, cops in this part of the world wore cowboy boots, whether dressing up or dressing down. They even wore them with their suits and to testify in court. Didn't matter if they'd ever laid eyes on a horse.

Seemed to be part of the uniform.

Ford might not be a cop anymore, but he sure looked the part, especially with his short, neat haircut and clean-shaven face.

"You could have come in," she said. "Instead of lurking outside, spying on us."

"I didn't want to interrupt. Besides, I wanted to observe you in your natural environment."

"What?" That surprised her. Why would he care about her art class? "You make me sound like a zoo specimen."

"I like to know who I'm working with," he said unapologetically.

Arnie, who moments ago had been friendly as a puppy, now stared at Ford with undisguised animosity. "This your squeeze?"

"Uh, no." Robyn laughed nervously. "Ford, this is Arnie Coombs. Arnie, Ford Hyatt. We're working on a project together."

Arnie ignored Ford's extended hand. "Huh. Dude looks like a cop to me."

Robyn hid her smile. It wouldn't do to show any kind of approval for Arnie's rudeness. But hadn't she just been thinking the same thing?

"Good instincts," Ford said. "I used to be a cop."

"Why're you not now?" Arnie wanted to know. Still hostile. Tense. Ready to spring.

"Arnie," Robyn interrupted. "If you're going to question the man, the least you could do is shake his hand."

He backed up. "Ain't shakin' hands with no cop."

Oh, boy. "Okay, kids, you can go. I'll see you on Thursday for the great unveiling of your finished pieces."

They didn't waste time making a break for freedom. All but Arnie, who continued to stare malevolently at Ford.

"You better not be bothering Ms. Jasperson," he said. Then his friend grabbed him by his oversize shirt and dragged him toward the door, muttering something about teacher's pet.

"Charming student you got there," Ford said dryly. "Are they all that polite?"

Robyn winced. "Around cops? Yeah. Arnie's never seen a cop's good side in his life." She knew just how he felt, too. Cops didn't exactly leave her warm and fuzzy.

"He's got a gang tattoo," Ford said. "Some of those

other kids were wearing colors. I thought gang colors were banned at most schools."

"They are, and during the regular school year they'd be sent home. But I don't make a big deal out of it in the summer. As long as they aren't killing each other in my classroom, they can wear what they want."

She straightened a few things on her desk, locked up her grade book and some other papers.

"Are you the only one here? The only adult, I mean."

"Usually. Well, there's the security guy. Why?" She picked up the tote bag that contained her change of clothes.

"I didn't see any guard. In fact, I walked right into the school unchallenged. I could be an ax murderer."

Robyn sighed. "You sound like my ex-mother-in-law. She never approved of me teaching at a public school. 'You take your life in your hands every day you associate with *those* people.'" She stuck her nose in the air and sniffed.

"It's not a matter of snobbery," he said firmly. "It's a safety issue. I've seen the violence gang members—"

"These kids aren't going to hurt me. You treat them like wild animals, they'll behave that way. If you treat them like human beings—"

Robyn looked up at his implacable face and realized she was preaching to a closed door. It wasn't the first time she'd faced this attitude. During her high school kangaroo court, he'd been just as determined to believe he already knew the truth about everything.

"Never mind," she said as she walked toward the door. She turned off the lights. Ford was there to open the door for her, an oddly gallant gesture given they were having an argument. But he'd always had nice manners. She remembered that about him.

"You said you've got some new information?" she asked as she locked the door. The jangle of her keys echoed in the empty hallway.

"I located Heather."

"You did?" she asked excitedly, their argument forgotten. "Where is she? Have you talked to her? Will she back up Eldon's story? Will she testify? Oh, my gosh, this is great!"

"Let's not get ahead of ourselves. I know where she lives. But she might refuse to talk to us. She might deny everything."

"Even if she knows a man's life is at stake?"

Ford looked uncomfortable. "I've seen people say and do some pretty heartless things to protect their own self-interest. It seems Heather has gone to considerable trouble to divorce herself from her life in Green Prairie. She might not appreciate that past coming back to haunt her."

Robyn stuck her keys in her purse. "Then we'll just have to convince her. Where is she? Is that where we're going?"

Ford nodded as they headed for the exit. Calvin, the elderly security guard, was walking down the hall toward them. He nodded and tipped an imaginary hat toward Robyn. "You take care now, Ms. Jasperson. It's hot out there."

"Thanks, Calvin, I will."

Calvin gave Ford a suspicious once-over, but didn't ask about him. Poor Ford. He'd probably never gotten so much as a parking ticket and suddenly everyone was looking at him like he was some kind of serial killer.

CHAPTER FIVE

FORD PULLED UP TO THE CURB in front of Heather Brinks's home, and for a few moments he and Robyn studied it silently.

It had taken them almost three hours to get to the small town of Ardmore, Louisiana. Since Robyn had confessed to skipping lunch, they had made only a brief stop for fast food. Ford had meant what he said about keeping their strength up. Already he could see that this fight was taking a toll on Robyn. He'd had to remind her several times to finish her hamburger.

During most of the trip, she'd sat in the passenger seat, tense and silent. Every once in a while she had shifted in her seat, curling one or the other leg under her as if she couldn't get comfortable.

He was relieved they'd finally arrived at their destination.

Heather Boone Brinks was married to the minister of a Lutheran church. She'd changed her name even before marrying, however. According to her high school friend, after leaving Green Prairie, Heather had sought refuge with one of her mother's former boyfriends and had started using his last name.

Robyn finally broke the silence. "I guess Heather

did pretty well for herself." She sounded both pleased and maybe a little resentful.

Ford still wasn't sure he'd made the right decision, bringing Robyn along. Just the sight of her—the ex-wife of the man with whom she'd been having an affair—might cause Heather to clam up. On the other hand, Heather and Robyn had once shared a rapport. Robyn was perhaps one of the first people to show a real interest in the girl, to encourage her.

Heather's large ranch-style house screamed conservative respectability, right down to the neutral paint colors and the white picket fence. She had cardinals painted on her mailbox, and a welcome wreath complete with little geese nailed to the front door.

"What was she like before?" Ford realized he should have questioned Robyn earlier.

"A mess," Robyn answered. "She was in the first art class I ever taught at the high school. Too pretty for her own good, big hair and big boobs, too much makeup. *Lots* of boyfriends."

"Promiscuous?"

"Ohhh, yeah."

"Good art student?"

Robyn laughed. "No. She could barely draw a stick figure. But she liked me okay. I'd been like her, in a way, when I was her age. Low self-esteem. Problems at home. Discipline issues her whole life. Looking for love in all the wrong places. I tried to reach out to her, and she seemed to respond. She poured herself into every art project, and even though the results weren't too good, I gave her an A.

"I used to go home and tell Eldon all about her. I thought I was making a difference."

"You were. Seems Heather landed on her feet."

"Yeah, after she had an affair with a married man. It still shocks me—not that Heather would sleep with an older, wealthy married man, but that Eldon would have sex with her when he knew how potentially damaging it would be to a fragile girl like her."

"Fragile?"

"Definitely. She was so caught up in what people thought of her. She once burst into tears when I gave her some instruction. You know, constructive stuff, like how to get a more realistic texture in the tree she was painting. Something really innocuous. I had to walk on eggshells around her."

That was bad news. If Heather Boone still cared a lot about what people thought of her, she would never admit to an illicit affair with a convicted child murderer.

Still, Robyn's presence here might be useful. She might be able to spot inconsistencies in her former student's story—if they could get her to tell any kind of story at all.

"I hope she's toughened up a little. Because Heather could bust this case wide open."

Robyn didn't seem convinced. "She'll make Eldon look like a liar. And everyone will see he was a phil-anderer."

"If she backs up Eldon's story, all of that won't matter. The police think Eldon killed Justin, then spent hours disposing of the body and setting up the fake kidnapping. But if Heather saw the child alive and well only minutes before his disappearance, the police would have to come up with a new theory. Eldon would have had less than ten minutes to kill the child and dispose of his body before—oh, God, Robyn, I'm sorry."

Robyn had flinched and turned away, covering her face with her hands.

Ford couldn't believe what a jerk he was. "I got caught up in the moment," he said, knowing it wouldn't help. "I forgot who I was talking to." He'd been thinking of Robyn as a colleague, an ally. He'd forgotten she was also the mother of a murdered little boy.

He couldn't imagine what she must have gone through. To nurture a child for more than two years, to have held him and hugged him and loved him, to have watched his first steps and heard his first words. And then to have him snatched away so cruelly...

Ford was no stranger to grief. His loss hadn't been as horrifying as Robyn's, true. But he should be able to at least relate to Robyn's grief. He shouldn't have been so careless.

"Robyn." He felt an alien urge to gather her in his arms and hold her, to kiss away her pain, pain that he had caused. He settled instead for smoothing a strand of her blond hair behind her ear. She'd worn it loose.

When she'd ducked into the girls' bathroom at school to change her clothes, she'd also taken down her hair and brushed it until it gleamed like burnished gold.

He liked it that way.

She didn't shy away from his touch, at least.

"I'm sorry. My ex-wife always said I was a callous bastard, and I guess she was right. I'll try to be a little more sensitive."

She dashed away a tear. "It's okay, really. It's nothing I haven't heard a zillion times. It's just that I thought I'd recovered. That I'd moved on. But seeing Eldon and remembering that awful night, that phone call at three o'clock in the morning…well, it's just all come rushing back."

"Why don't you wait in the car while I talk to Heather," he said, unwilling to submit her to any more painful reminders.

"I want to be there. I know I can get through to her. Please, Ford."

She was leaving the decision up to him. He deliberated another moment or two before giving in. "All right. But follow my lead, okay? I'm good at this."

She nodded her agreement.

"You know, we can't discount Heather as a suspect. If she had mur—if she were guilty of a crime, would Eldon protect her?"

"Ford, please, don't guard your words. I'm okay now. Would Eldon protect her if she had killed his child? Absolutely not. But *she* could have snatched Justin out of the car. No one saw her that night after…

after it happened, including Eldon. She could have driven him anyplace and…well, you know. The fact that she left town and changed her name is suspicious."

Ford nodded. "Maybe Heather saw herself as the next Mrs. Jasperson, but she didn't fancy being a stepmother. Eldon said she wasn't comfortable around Justin."

"Exactly. Let's go get her."

Robyn stood a bit to the side on the front porch as Ford rang the bell. He didn't want Heather to see her until she'd opened the door.

The door opened after a few moments, and a young woman spoke to them through the screen door. "Yes?"

Ford had to squint to be sure. The woman looked very little like her old driver's license picture. But this was indeed Heather Boone. Her long, wavy, bleached-blond hair was now a medium brown, cut into a neat, short cap. Instead of a load of black eyeliner and long, dangly earrings, her face was clean of makeup, and she wore tiny gold studs on her earlobes.

Her dress looked as if it had been sewn out of someone's flowered curtains. High-necked, with puffy sleeves and a white collar, it looked like something his mother would have worn.

"Hello, ma'am," Ford said, ultrapolite. "My name is Ford Hyatt, and I need to talk to you about a matter of some urgency. You are Heather Boone, is that correct?"

Her eyes widened slightly at the mention of her real maiden name, but she quickly covered the reaction. "I don't need any insurance," she said primly, starting to close the door.

"Wait. I'm not selling anything. I'm here to talk about Eldon Jasperson. I think you might have some information that can save his life."

At the mention of Eldon's name, the door stopped moving. "I don't know any Eldon Jasperson," she said cautiously.

"Well, now, I'm sure that if you think back, you'll remember him. One of the richest men from your hometown? Green Prairie, Texas?"

"I've never...been—I haven't heard of it."

"You were born there, Heather." Robyn stepped into view, obviously unable to stand in the shadows another moment. "You spent the first eighteen years of your life there."

Heather's eyes widened in alarm.

"Please," Robyn said, "we aren't here to cause trouble for you. You have some information that might prove Eldon's innocence. You might not even know you have it."

Heather shook her head. "I don't know anything. Please leave."

"Why? Are you afraid the neighbors will see us and ask questions?" Ford asked. "Are you afraid we'll spoil whatever little fiction you've concocted about your past? Does your husband know about the drugs, and all those men back in—"

"Shh!" Heather hissed. "My son is in the next room."

Ford didn't lower his voice at all. "Well, if you don't want your son to know you were a slut and a drug addict, you'll talk to us."

"Ford!" Robyn objected, but he gave her a warning look that quelled any further outbursts. He knew his tactics were harsh sometimes, but he'd learned to get results. Anyway, Heather was lying and he didn't like liars—or people who covered their own asses without regard to anyone else.

"All right, fine," Heather said. "I'll give you five minutes. But this is ridiculous. I don't know anything." She quickly scanned the street before ushering them inside, probably wondering if any neighbors were peeking out their windows.

Small towns were like that. Everybody had to know everybody else's business. He'd been relieved when he'd moved out of Green Prairie to Houston and could live in relative anonymity.

Once inside the house, he could see what he hadn't discerned through the screen: Heather was pregnant, close to term if he was any judge.

She showed them into a formal living room, furnished in stiff brocade furniture, about as inviting as a funeral home.

Just as they sat down, a little boy appeared in the doorway, staring curiously. He was about three, with thick, tousled hair and a juice mustache. A ragged stuffed animal of unidentifiable species dangled from one hand. "Mommy, who that?"

Robyn stared at the child with a yearning so palpable it filled the room. Damn it! This kid wasn't much older than Justin had been when he disappeared. Did the woman need any more reminders?

Heather quickly scooped up her son. "No one you need to worry about," she muttered as she swept him out of the room.

Ford couldn't look at Robyn. He wanted to say something but didn't dare, positive he'd say exactly the wrong thing. He wasn't good at warm fuzzies.

Heather returned a short time later. She settled into a tufted, velvet-upholstered chair: a large, imposing marble-top table separated her from Ford and Robyn on the hard sofa.

"Would you like something to drink?" she said, a good Southern hostess despite everything.

"No, thank you," Ford and Robyn said together.

"Heather, don't waste our time with more lies, okay? We know exactly where you were the night Justin Jasperson was kidnapped. We need to hear your side of the story."

"As I said, I don't know what you're talking about. I was a kid when that happened."

"So where were you?"

She shrugged. "I don't remember. Probably home, asleep."

"Okay then, let me ask you this. What kind of pizza do you like?"

The question rattled her for a moment, but she quickly composed herself. "I don't see what that has to do with anything."

"Humor me."

"We don't eat much pizza. Brad, my husband, considers it junk food. I prepare most of our meals at home."

"But you must have eaten pizza when you were in high school. What high school kid doesn't? So what kind did you like?"

"I don't remember. Sausage."

"Not pepperoni and black olive?"

Heather schooled her face into a neutral expression. "I don't know—"

"Damn it, Heather, are you so wrapped up in your new life with your respectable husband and your perfect children that you would let an innocent man die to protect your lie?"

"I'm not lying!"

"So you weren't having sex with a married man while his wife was out of town?"

"No! I don't know Eldon Jasperson. Never met the man."

"Heather," Robyn said quietly, "that's a lie. You met him when you were my student. He came to the Arts Fair at the school. He bought one of your paintings."

"If he did, I don't remember."

Robyn glanced over at Ford and shook her head slightly.

"I know, you don't owe me anything," Ford continued. "But what about Mrs. Jasperson? She had faith
in you when no one else did. She helped you through
some tough times. She saw you as a person, instead
of someone to be used and tossed aside. And yet you
won't lift a finger to help her.

"So long as Eldon Jasperson sits in jail, the person
who stole her son from her remains free to commit
more crimes."

"Obviously I would help if I could," Heather said
flatly.

Ford had to do something to shake Heather out of
her deep pattern of denial.

"Heather," Ford said quietly, "it's not just that
Eldon claims you were with him that night. He has
security cameras all over his house. He has footage
of you arriving at his house that night." Ford made
up the story as he went along. "He put it on a CD and
stored it in a safe-deposit box. He never intended to
use it unless he had no other choice."

It was a stupid story. If such evidence existed, it
would have been found long before now. But Heather
didn't think it through. Her face registered alarm,
then panic.

"I want you out of this house right now. You leave,
or I'll call the police."

Robyn scrambled to her feet, but Ford sat right
where he was, wanting to show Heather that her
threats didn't scare him. "Okay. You sit here in your
pretty little house and let everyone keep believing

you're a pious, God-fearing woman who goes to church and gives to charity and volunteers at the nursing home. But you must have a heart of stone if you can kiss your little boy good-night and not think about Ms. Jasperson, and the fact that she doesn't have a little boy anymore. That someone killed him and you're letting him walk around free."

Now Ford stood, but only so he could get in Heather's face. "What if it were your child? What if someone took your son—"

Robyn grabbed her purse and fled the room. Moments later the front door slammed.

Heather's face crumpled, and for a moment, he thought he had her. But then she seemed to firm up her resolve. "Will you get out, please? I have heard quite enough."

"Sure. Say a prayer for me in church, okay? And better yet say one for yourself, too, because God doesn't let unrepentant liars into heaven."

ROBYN WAS STILL TREMBLING with outrage by the time Ford joined her in the car.

"You okay?" he asked as he started the engine.

"No, I'm not okay." She was perilously close to tears. One too many reminders of her loss had assaulted her today. Her nerves were so close to the surface, she was going to have a meltdown if Ford so much as hit a bump in the road.

"Want to go someplace, get some coffee or something?"

Caffeine. That was all she needed. "How could you do that?" she asked. "How could you use that woman's child against her? You don't have children, do you?"

"No."

"Then you have no idea how it feels. When you're a mother, you worry all the time. You worry when you're pregnant that the child will have something wrong when it's born. You worry that it won't survive your lack of parenting skills. Then you worry if someone else is taking care of him.

"And most of all, you worry someone will hurt him. Maybe even someone he loves and trusts. To have someone thrust that fear right in your face—you were practically threatening her!"

"I was using accepted interrogation techniques—"

"On a pregnant woman, with her child in the next room. She had no lawyer present, no one she could call for help. That was unconscionable."

"Robyn, look, I'm sorry if I upset you. But I am all about getting results. That woman is lying through her teeth."

"How do you know?"

"I can see it! You caught her in a blatant lie yourself."

"But she might be telling the truth about Eldon. We know Eldon—"

"She's not. She just doesn't want her husband to know about her sordid past."

"You cops—you're always so damn sure. You

sounded just like the detectives who questioned me after Justin disappeared. They cornered me in that stinking interrogation room for *hours* and they hammered me and hammered me. They came up with every sordid way I could have murdered my child, my heart, my flesh and blood for whom I would have gladly lain down and died a thousand times—"

Now, she did cry. The storm that had been brewing for days burst out of her. She'd never told anyone this, not even her closest friends. She'd felt she had to be strong, for Justin's sake.

"They acted like they had proof I did it. They asked the same questions over and over, and then they gave the answers, and all I had to do was nod my head and they would let me go home. And I was so tempted—so tempted to say yes, I did it, just so they would let me out of that room."

Ford pulled over to the side of the road. "I'm sorry the police did that to you. But it's how they operate. It's how guilty suspects are broken down. You have to manipulate their emotions."

"You say 'they' and 'them,' but they're your methods, too. Even in high school—same questions over and over. Same assumption of guilt."

He nodded, awarding her the point. "Unfortunately, innocent people like you do get caught up in those methods."

Ford found a box of tissue and handed it to her. She grabbed a wad and wiped at her face. "So you're willing to believe that maybe, just maybe, I didn't steal those art supplies?"

He looked away. "There certainly wasn't enough evidence to draw that conclusion."

"I'm asking what you believe. Not then, but now."

"Robyn, it was years ago."

She considered pressing him but she suspected she wouldn't like the answer she got. So she dropped it. Her innocence in a high school theft wasn't the point here.

"I shouldn't have brought you with me," he said. "This is too hard for you. And it's only going to get harder."

"No, please, don't shut me out." She pushed thoughts of the past out of her mind and sniffed back the last of her tears. "I'm okay now. No more breakdowns."

"I can't do this job if I'm constantly worried about hurting you. You're right, I can't possibly understand what you've gone through or how it feels to lose a child in such a terrible way. But you're wrong about one thing. I did lose a child."

CHAPTER SIX

SHE GASPED AND LOOKED at him sharply.

"My ex-wife had a miscarriage," he added hastily.

"Oh, God, I'm sorry."

"It's not the same as what you—"

"Oh, Ford, of course it's the same. Losing a child is a devastating loss no matter what the circumstances. Sometimes I tend to believe I'm the only one who has ever suffered. I get self-absorbed."

"Please, don't apologize. I didn't tell you that so you could feel sorry for me. I just don't want you to think of me as some heartless machine."

Robyn suddenly *did* see Ford in a different light. She'd known he had an ex-wife—he'd mentioned her once. But she'd never pictured him as a family man, as having any paternal inclinations at all. To her he was a means to an end, part of a justice machine that for once was going to work in her favor.

He wasn't heartless. He *was* focused on a goal. If he had to offend a selfish, dishonest minister's wife to save Eldon's life—even if she was some kid's mommy—wasn't that an acceptable trade-off?

With a start, Robyn realized Ford was touching her hair, as he'd done earlier when she'd freaked out about some damn thing. He probably thought she was a fragile little flower that he had to tiptoe around.

His touch felt way too good. Not exactly comforting, as he no doubt meant it to be. In fact, the heat of his big hand on her scalp made her want to squirm in her seat.

She reached up and took his hand, pulling it away from her hair. "I'm okay now." Her voice came out breathy, like Marilyn Monroe's. She didn't let go of his hand.

Afraid to look at him, afraid she would see her own sudden heat reflected in his eyes, she stared down at her lap.

She heard him unbuckle his seat belt, felt him slide across the big bench seat toward her. He slid one arm around her shoulders, and for a moment she thought he'd take her in his arms and kiss her. She kind of hoped he would.

But he pulled her against his shoulder instead. "I'm an insensitive bastard. I suck. But I'm not likely to change my ways. I know how to do my job and I'm good at it. Trust me."

"I do," she insisted.

"If you want to hang close, I won't stop you. But you have to promise me something."

"I won't break down again, I swear. It's just that—"

"I wasn't going to ask that of you," he said. "What I want you to promise is that you won't hold back. You won't stifle your feelings. If you're upset, let it out. Because I won't be able to sleep at night if I think you're going home alone and crying your eyes out because I trampled all over your feelings. If I act like a pigheaded clod, at least give me the chance to apologize for it."

She looked up at him. "Deal."

That was when she realized she did see something in his eyes, some flicker of desire, the twin to her own small flame that now burned even brighter.

Oh, no-no-no, this wouldn't do. She started to wiggle out of his grasp, then realized she had no-where to go. He had her pinned against the door.

They shared the same air, almost the same breath. In the span of a heartbeat, she no longer wanted to escape. In another heartbeat, she wanted his kiss more than oxygen.

It should have felt awkward as hell, but instead it felt like the exact right thing to do. They'd both bared their souls, at least a little. It seemed only fitting they punctuate their true confessions with a friendly kiss.

But this didn't feel merely friendly. She'd seen those old movie clichés of fireworks and waves crashing against rocks, but this was the first time she'd understood what those visual analogies meant.

Oh, God, he smelled good. The smell of his skin was intoxicating.

When his mouth finally made contact with hers, it was a sweet kiss, a gentle kiss, and Robyn didn't want it to end. But it did, all too quickly.

Ford eased away from her. "Um, yeah. That wasn't supposed to happen."

"Weak moment," Robyn agreed, then laughed nervously. "We can pretend it never did." As if she could put it out of her mind. No way. She wished she could bottle the way she felt right now, all tingly and warm and strangely right with the world.

Ford slid across the seat, resuming his spot behind the wheel. "I've wanted to do that ever since high school."

"Yeah, me, too."

He started the car. "You? The girl who so thoroughly snubbed me in the cafeteria, when all I wanted to do was help her study Shakespeare?"

"Oh, yeah. 'The Bard.'"

"God. You had to remind me what a pretentious ass I was. I rehearsed that opening line for ten minutes before I walked up to you. And you shot me down with a few icy words."

Robyn had a hard time believing him, then and now. He wasn't the only one who'd been crushing in high school. She'd been watching him at football practice for weeks, fantasizing about various improbable ways they could meet and get naked. But when he'd opened the door, she'd slammed it in his face, terrified that it was some kind of joke, that he would lure her into opening up, get past her defenses and find some vulnerability to exploit. People had been doing that all her life.

"I did behave rather badly," she admitted. "If you were sincere."

"I was."

"For what it's worth, I thought a lot about kissing you, too." Her face warmed, and she hoped he didn't look over at her, because she was sure her face was turning the shade of a ripe tomato.

Amazing how one potent memory could instantly make her feel like a gawky teenager again.

Ford glanced over at her, studying her out of the corner of his eye. "Huh."

"Well, now we've satisfied our curiosity. Back to business."

"Right." He cleared his throat and made a big deal of refastening his seat belt. "I didn't tell you about the wig fiber." He started up the car and launched a detailed explanation of what the Project Justice evidence analyst had found. Robyn didn't understand half of it—science had never been her forte. She understood the gist of it, though. They had a small chance at tracking down that wig.

But she had a hard time focusing on the specifics of how, when and why. Her mind was on that kiss.

She hadn't dated since she'd lost Justin. In fact, she hadn't experienced so much as a passing urge toward any man until she'd seen Ford again. The part of her that connected with others on an intimate level had died along with her son. She'd believed that her students satisfied any emotional needs she might have;

she poured her heart and soul into reaching those kids and being a positive influence in their lives.

Apparently she'd been wrong. Something inside her, long asleep, had awakened—at a damned inconvenient time, too. She wished she had someone to talk to, but she simply didn't have any close female friends.

It was going to be a long drive back to Green Prairie.

THE CALLER ID TOLD ROBYN it was Ford calling. She glanced at the clock and realized she had slept much later than normal.

Her heart pounding, she picked up the phone, anxious to hear his voice. Yesterday had ended on a strange, awkward note when he'd dropped her off at the school parking lot to pick up her car. He'd waited to see that she got safely into her car and that it started, his concern for her welfare warming her heart.

But nothing had been said; he'd made no further reference to the kiss, when it was all she could think about. She had said they could pretend it hadn't happened, but was he even capable of that? She certainly wasn't.

"Hello, Ford," she said, trying to inject just the right note of cordiality into her voice.

"Hi. Are you up for some strictly unglamorous phone work?" He explained about calling the wig retailers, and she was all for it.

"I'm ready to do anything other than sit and wait for the phone to ring."

"This is normally the kind of thing we get our college interns to do," he said, still apologizing. "But one of them is sick, and the other two are already committed to helping with another case."

"I don't mind, really," she assured him.

"Can you bring Trina with you? I know she's angry, but we need her on the team. The more people we have working on this, the more ground we can cover. And we have a lot of ground."

"I'll see what I can do," Robyn had promised.

So she called and made nice to Trina, who had sounded strained, but less emotional.

"If Ford wants me there, I guess I should go," she'd said. "But I'm not happy with the direction he's going."

"He knows what he's doing," Robyn assured her. "Besides, what we're doing today has nothing to do with…with what we talked about the other day. We're going to help with that wig fiber."

"Okay. I'll pick you up in a few minutes."

"I can drive. You drove last time."

"No offense, Robyn, but if we're going to drive on Houston freeways, I'd rather be in my car. It's bigger and safer. And I need my lumbar support."

"Your air-conditioning probably works better than mine anyway," Robyn said, unsure why Trina's request irked her. Trina liked to be in control, that was one thing. She was always the center of attention during meetings with lawyers.

Then again, it was *her* husband they were trying to save, not Robyn's. Perhaps Trina should be running the show.

They said little during the hour-long drive. Robyn had struggled to get a conversation going, carefully avoiding the subject of Eldon's infidelity, but after a while the effort had been too much, and they'd lapsed into silence, letting a Christina Aguilera CD fill the car instead.

The blatantly romantic, sexy music made Robyn think of Ford again. She couldn't get that kiss out of her mind. And though she knew it didn't mean anything, that spur-of-the-moment embrace that had caught them both unawares, she couldn't help the way her body responded every time she thought of Ford, which was about every thirty seconds or so.

Totally inappropriate on her part. She was trying to save a man's life, and personal feelings would only get in the way of that goal.

So long as she didn't act on her feelings—act again—she supposed it didn't do any harm to fantasize. Sometimes she needed the distraction. When her revived grief threatened to swamp her, she would just think about Ford's lips on hers or the feel of his hand smoothing her hair, and any threatening tears would back off.

Trina pulled into a parking spot on Main Street near Project Justice, which was housed in a landmark building in the historic district. After feeding the meter some quarters, they stood on the sidewalk, staring at the imposing edifice. It was three stories of red brick with cream-colored masonry trim around the doors and gracefully arched windows. Two wide stone steps led up to the oak double doors, bracketed by a pair of old copper-sheathed gaslights.

Robyn thought it was one of the most beautiful buildings in the whole city. Houston was a relatively new city, and few of its early structures had been saved.

"I wonder why they chose this old place," Trina said. "The guy who started Project Justice has millions, doesn't he?"

Robyn shrugged. "Maybe they like it here." She climbed the steps, unwilling to argue taste with Trina. But Trina stopped her with a hand to her arm.

"Listen, before we go in there, I just want to say I'm sorry for the way I acted, storming out of the meeting that way. You just shocked me, that's all."

Robyn knew how it felt, so she just nodded.

"I can't believe Eldon was unfaithful to me," she said, jutting her chin forward belligerently. "But I want to know—what else is Ford going to hit me with? If there are going to be any unpleasant bombshells, I'd like advance warning."

Ford had wanted to tell Trina about their interview with Eldon, but Robyn had thought it best not to bring it up. So long as Heather flatly denied knowing Eldon, she was no good to their case anyway.

"Are you sure you want to know?" Robyn asked.

Trina folded her arms and leaned against the brick wall. "What now?" In her hot-pink jeans and hand-painted silk tank top, she could have been posing for a fashion photo.

"Eldon confirmed that there was a woman. We located her in Louisiana. She's a minister's wife, and she denied everything."

"You see there?" Trina said, latching onto anything that might bolster her case. "Your mystery woman is a preacher's wife, not some husband-stealing bimbo."

The irony of that statement was apparently lost on Trina, who'd just described herself, but Robyn of course let it pass. She'd never confronted Trina about her affair with Eldon while he was still married, because she'd always figured, what would it help?

But sometimes Trina made it so tempting.

"Whatever Eldon told you," Trina continued, "he was probably just yanking your chain, or grasping at straws. He's desperate, you know. Who wouldn't be?"

"You're probably right," Robyn said. Trina's reaction only cemented her opinion that Trina shouldn't be told everything—whether she had a right to the information or not.

Project Justice occupied the entire building. Robyn immediately felt the energy of the place when she walked into the foyer, with its tall ceiling, polished wood floors and grand chandelier. A frosted glass screen separated the foyer from the rest of the first floor, but through it, Robyn saw the shadows of people moving about and heard the muted voices of those working beyond her vision.

On one wall was a large gold seal, the Project Justice logo. Around it were framed newspaper clippings describing the various successes the foundation boasted. How many innocent men and women had been freed because of Ford's work, and that of his colleagues? A more sobering thought was, how many more were still imprisoned because no one had championed their cause?

Then her gaze settled on the receptionist, and she froze to the floor. The woman had to be seventy-five if she was a day, but she was no sweet little old lady. She had a mane of long, curly silver hair, bright purple glasses, red lipstick and gigantic, dangly red rhinestone earrings.

As she set aside her *Soldier of Fortune* magazine, the look she gave Robyn and Trina could only be described as an imposing glare.

"May I help you?" Her booming voice made the word *help* sound like a curse.

"I'm, um, Robyn Jasperson." Robyn hated the tremor in her voice. She had every right to be here— had been invited here. So why did this woman terrify her? "Ford Hyatt invited me, er, us, to come here."

"Hmph," said the woman, whose nameplate identified her as Celeste. "Show me ID."

Robyn reached obediently into her purse. She had a "scary teacher voice" that she used when any student gave her trouble, and usually it made them jump to obey. But she wasn't used to anyone using that technique on her.

Trina didn't appear at all cowed. She stepped forward and Robyn braced herself. Part of her wanted to watch these two women tangle. But only a small, evil part of her. A conflict would slow them down.

"We're here to help on an important case. Don't you recognize us?"

Celeste eyed Trina up and down. "Can't say as I do. That's why I asked for ID. I'm not singling you out, you know. Boss's orders. No one gets through here without showing me ID."

Robyn handed over her driver's license. "Just do it, Trina."

"Oh, all right." Trina pouted and made a production out of pulling everything from her tiny purse before finding a slim wallet and a driver's license.

Celeste studied the IDs, then the women, with a critical eye. "You two are related?"

"No, we—" Robyn started, but Trina interrupted.

"Can you just call Ford Hyatt, please? We're on a tight schedule."

"I'll do that." Celeste relinquished the licenses, setting them on the polished marble counter between them with long, elegant hands. Her nails were painted bright red.

Trina reclaimed her license and restuffed her purse, her short, jerky movements broadcasting her irritation. Robyn reminded herself to cut Trina some slack. She had to be beside herself with anxiety over her husband.

Celeste gave Trina a sour look before picking up the phone and dialing an extension. "Mr. Hyatt, two *ladies* here to see you. Both seem to be Ms. Jasperson."

She listened a moment, then hung up. "Apparently you were expected," she said as if she hadn't believed their story and was surprised to find it true. "Mr. Hyatt will be here shortly to escort you back." She handed each of them a visitor tag. "Wear these in plain sight while you're here, or you're apt to be thrown out on your tushies. And don't wander the building without an escort."

Robyn resisted the urge to click her heels and salute.

She was relieved when Ford appeared from behind the screen a few moments later, offering them a brief, welcoming smile. Today he was casual in a Rice University football T-shirt that accented his wide shoulders, the soft cotton draping over his pecs. Faded jeans hugged his thighs, and his beat-up Converse All Stars made her think of pickup basketball in the park, playing Shirts and Skins. Mostly skins.

But he looked like he'd been putting in long hours. He hadn't shaved, and his somber expression meant he probably hadn't made any more progress.

She longed to reach out to him, to touch him, connect with him on some physical level. When had she let herself get so obsessed with Ford and his delectable body? It was a dangerous preoccupation, one she needed to shelve. She couldn't allow Ford to become distracted by misplaced sexual urges. She needed him one hundred percent focused on this case.

A man's life depended on that.

CHAPTER SEVEN

SHE HAD TO FORCE HERSELF not to lock gazes with him.

"Thank you for coming on such short notice." He opened the almost-invisible door in the glass screen. "This way. Do you want a quick tour of the offices?"

"I'd really like to get started," Trina said. "I have a dentist appointment at three."

This was the first Robyn had heard about an appointment. She was annoyed that Trina hadn't mentioned it, but she didn't want to argue with the woman, so again she said nothing.

"I'll just point things out as we pass, then," Ford said coolly, but he gave Robyn a look that said the comment wasn't aimed at her.

"What's the deal with that woman out front?" Trina asked as they followed Ford down the hall, apparently unaware of her own rudeness. "She's offensive."

"Ah, Celeste. She's our resident pit bull. Fiercely protective. She discourages casual visitors, who only waste our time."

"She could discourage the National Guard," Trina

mumbled. "How much do you pay her to sit out there, read magazines and scare the hell out of people?"

"You'd have to ask her. But whatever her salary, she earns it. She has a sharp mind, wasted during forty years as a Houston patrol officer. She wanted to be a detective but couldn't get herself promoted."

"Sexism?" Robyn asked.

"More like Celeste-ism. She always managed to piss off whoever was doing the promoting."

Robyn could see that.

"Any news on the case?" Trina asked. "It's such a shame Eldon doesn't have an alibi."

Robyn wanted to smack her. She was fishing for information she already had, testing Ford to see if he would tell her.

"We can talk more when we get to the boiler room."

True to his word, he pointed out things as they passed. "That's the bull pen," he said as they walked by a large, open area of cubicles. "Project Justice employs a handful of senior investigators who oversee all of the cases, with offices upstairs. Each senior investigator has four to six cases at a time, which is a much smaller load than most city detectives. The foundation has more manpower and money devoted per case than most police departments can afford, which means every lead gets investigated."

Robyn noticed that he did not include himself in his explanations—as if he was no longer a part of

Project Justice, but more of a guest. Apparently he hadn't changed his mind about his resignation.

They peeked in the door of the foundation's small laboratory, where several white-coated employees worked at microscopes or other futuristic-looking machines.

The company had a nicely appointed lunchroom, where a catering company was setting out a sandwich buffet.

"If I worked here I'd be big as a house," Trina said, eyeing a huge bowl that contained packages of M&M's for the taking.

"Help yourself to anything. The fridge is full of any kind of drink you could want. Coffee's over there in the corner. Daniel believes his people can't think clearly if they're hungry, so he makes sure they aren't."

"Wow, nice boss," Trina said.

The boiler room was a large, open room with a U-shaped table practically filling the whole space. On the table were at least a dozen telephones, blank legal pads, pens, clean, empty glasses and pitchers of ice water.

Two women sat at one end, working the phones, speaking in quiet, businesslike voices.

"This is where we're going to work?" Trina asked, wrinkling her nose.

"I warned you it wouldn't be glamorous. I need each of you to take a seat and grab a phone." He placed a packet of papers stapled together on the table in front of each of them. "These are all the wig shops within a hundred-mile radius of Green Prairie."

"That's a lot of wig shops," Trina murmured, leafing through the papers.

"I've also included every place I could find that sells wigs over the internet. What we're looking for is a shop that was open eight years ago and that carried Brandenburg wigs in the Allure line. So you'll want to talk to a manager, or an employee who's been there a long time."

He continued with the instructions—what to ask, how to follow up, what to write down, where to ask the shops to send receipts or forward computer records. Robyn took notes while Trina fidgeted.

"What are the chances?" Trina asked. "I mean, don't most businesses throw out that stuff after five years?"

"An astounding number of people keep everything. Yeah, the chances are very slim that this will pay off. However, until we have something better—"

"This is it, then?" Trina asked. "Saving my husband's life rests on this very slim chance that we can find out who bought that wig? What about the witness? Why can't you find this Roy guy?"

Robyn sighed quietly. So far, Trina had proved herself more of a liability than an asset.

"I've been going over the handwritten notes of the responding officer. There was, in fact, a Roy mentioned there who was not later interviewed."

"Do you have a last name?" Robyn asked excitedly.

"Actually, yes. Roy White. Ring any bells?"

Trina looked blank, and Robyn shook her head. "I don't remember that name ever coming up. There was a White family that lived on Cherry Street. His father drove a cement truck, I think."

Ford scribbled notes. "That could help. It's possible this man saw something that didn't gibe with Eldon being the guilty party, so the police quietly removed it from the file. I've seen stuff like that happen."

"That's awful," Trina said. "But White is such a common name. Do you think you might actually find this guy?"

"I'll try."

"We better get to work, too," Robyn said. She didn't really like talking on the phone, asking people to do things for her. She once volunteered for a charity fund drive where she had to call dozens and dozens of people and ask them for money. It had been excruciating.

But she would do what she had to do.

"Make notes about every single call you make," Ford said. "If they don't want to help you, appeal to their sympathies. Tell them you need them to save an innocent man's life. Tell them they could help put a child killer behind bars. Hell, tell them they'll be on a reality TV show. Wheedle, cry, whatever it takes to get their cooperation."

Ah. Robyn saw now the real reason he'd asked them to perform this particular task. It would be much harder to say no to a woman who was about to be a widow, or another who'd lost her child, than to deny some anonymous employee of a foundation they'd never heard of.

Whatever worked.

TWO HOURS INTO HER TASK, Robyn was ready to admit defeat. Her back hurt, her ear was sore and she was going hoarse. She'd been cursed out in three languages, hung up on and generally treated like a lowlife telemarketer interrupting someone's dinner.

So when she actually got a sympathetic person on the phone, a woman who'd owned her wig shop for twenty years, who had sold Brandenburg Allure wigs and who had kept all of her sales records, Robyn almost fell out of her chair.

"I remember that trial," the woman said. "I watched it on truTV. Such a tragedy. And you're… the wife?"

"The ex-wife, actually," Robyn said. "But I know in my heart that my ex-husband did not harm our son. The police rushed to judgment. Evidence was overlooked and clues weren't followed. You would help me so much if you could just send me copies of your sales receipts from that year."

The woman chuckled. "Truth be told, I was just

getting ready to clean out that storeroom and throw out all those old papers. I'll just send 'em your way, how about that?"

"Great. Thank you so much."

"What's your address, honey?"

Robyn was so shocked by the woman's cooperation that she forgot to give the Project Justice mailing address, and instead rattled off her home address.

She started to correct herself, then figured, oh, well, she could give the package to Ford when she received it. When she hung up, she realized Trina had been listening to the exchange.

"How many is that for you?" Trina asked.

"Actually, that's the first shop that's offered to send me receipts. How about you?"

"I've got three," Trina said. "Try crying. It really works."

"I'll remember that," Robyn said dryly. "But this isn't a competition."

Trina instantly sobered. "Sorry. I don't mean to be frivolous. But this is the most god-awful boring job. I was just trying to make it a little bit fun."

Robyn couldn't help it—she smiled at Trina, who was sometimes very childlike. Eldon had described her as exuberant, full of life, funny. Robyn hadn't seen that side of her, but maybe there was more to Trina than met the eye. Maybe she was one of those people who had to warm up to you before you could see their best qualities.

"You're right," Robyn said. "There's no reason we have to treat *everything* so deadly serious."

"Next yes I get, I'm going to reward myself with another package of M&M's."

"Unless I get there first."

Robyn decided to try the internet wig shops. Most of them, she discovered, had not had an online presence eight years ago, so it was easy to eliminate them. She found one that had been selling wigs in cyberspace for twelve years. All of their records were on computer, and the man she talked to agreed to send the pertinent receipts. Robyn didn't resort to crying, either, though she would have.

"Score one more for the home team," she said.

"Good work," Trina said. "Oh, crap, I gotta leave for my dentist appointment. It takes months to get an appointment with this guy, but he supposedly does the best crowns in all of Houston."

"Oh…"

"Don't tell me you want to stay and do more of this."

"Well, someone has to. I was just hitting my stride. I finally figured out what to say and how to say it so that I don't get hung up on."

Ford walked in just then, and Robyn drank in the sight of him. Did she really want to keep making these uncomfortable calls, or did she just want to hang around Ford? She was pathetically transparent, even to herself.

"How are you ladies doing?"

"We're kickin' ass," Trina said.

Robyn shrugged. "We're making some progress."

"Good." Ford rubbed his hands together with relish. "You'll both be happy to know, I found Roy White, thanks to your tip about the cement truck, Robyn. He's living in Bozeman, Montana. He said the police interviewed him that night. He saw something he thought was important, but no one followed up on it. Then his army reserve unit shipped out to Afghanistan, and he didn't think anymore of it."

"Well, what did he see?" Robyn asked. Surely if this mystery witness had implicated Eldon, Ford wouldn't look or sound so animated.

"He wouldn't say. I think he was angling to get paid for the information. He knows Eldon has money."

"*Had* money," Trina said sullenly. "The legal fees have eaten through most of his assets. And that house costs a bundle to maintain. I've already got a second mortgage on it."

"What about his mother?" Ford asked.

Trina barked a laugh. "Ha. Tightwad Tillie? She quit giving money to the cause years ago—hardly even speaks to me. I think she believes her own son is guilty."

Robyn nodded. Ever since Eldon's father had died a few years ago, Tillie Jasperson had tried to sweep Eldon's very existence under the carpet. It was like she wished it would all go away. She seemed embarrassed by her two daughters-in-law.

Trina looked at her watch again. "I have *got* to go." She self-consciously gathered up all her candy wrappers and tossed them into a trash can.

"I can take this list home with me," Robyn said to Ford, "and make more calls from there."

"I'd prefer you keep working at the call center, so we have an official record of your calls, and you have the ability to record conversations if you need to. If transportation is the problem, I can run you home later."

"Run me home? It's forty miles."

"I don't mind."

"He doesn't mind," Trina said. "I think you should stay." Behind Ford's back, she waggled her eyebrows at Robyn.

Oh, great. All she needed was for Trina to start playing matchmaker, or dropping hints, or gossiping about an imagined romance between her and Ford.

Still, if Trina sensed something...

Trina collected her bundle of papers and handed a much-scribbled-upon legal pad to Ford. "Let me know what else I can do. I can see myself out." She strode out of the room, blatantly violating Celeste's orders.

Ford watched her go, looking perplexed. "I'll just make sure she gets out safely."

"Afraid Celeste will body-tackle her?" Robyn was only half kidding.

Robyn made another fruitless call. When she hung up, she discovered Ford was standing behind her.

"I didn't want to interrupt." He took the chair Trina had vacated. "Was it a mistake including Trina?" He studied the mostly illegible notes.

"She actually had better luck than I did. She's very persuasive on the phone. I mostly got cursed out and hung up on."

Ford looked at Robyn's list. "But you got a few of the shops to agree to send receipts?"

"A few."

"That's a few more than we had yesterday. Who knows, maybe we'll get lucky. Did you eat lunch?"

"What time is it?"

"Almost two o'clock. And I'll take that as a no. There's a great Mexican place around the corner. Best carne asada you ever had in your life."

Robyn realized she was starving. "Okay. Pardon me for bringing this up, but you seem kind of… chipper."

His eyebrows flew up. "Do I?"

"Quite a bit different than the man I found in a dive bar, drowning his sorrows."

Ford immediately sobered. "I was having a bad day."

"Hey, didn't mean to bring you down."

Ford's brows knitted in thought. "It's the thrill of the hunt, I guess. When I'm on a case, I get kind of hyper. The fact that I drink way too much coffee doesn't help."

"I wasn't complaining. Just…noticing."

"Did you say yes to Mexican food?"

She hadn't answered one way or another, but she had to eat. The sandwiches in the lunchroom were probably dried out by now, if they hadn't all been eaten. And she couldn't stomach one more bite of M&Ms. She'd almost kept pace with Trina.

"Bring it on."

Ten minutes later, they were seated at Casa Milagro, eating chips and spicy queso and sipping from tall glasses of iced tea while they waited for their lunches to arrive.

The waitress brought their meals, and for a few minutes they didn't talk, they just ate. Despite Ford's resounding recommendation of the carne asada, Robyn had ordered chicken sour-cream enchiladas.

She couldn't remember the last time she had any kind of real appetite for food. Once the steaming platter was in front of her, the scent made her mouth water. She didn't even wait for it to cool down. She cut off a bite of enchilada and blew on it a couple of times, then popped it into her mouth and sighed.

It was good. The food was so good, in fact, that twice she caught herself actually moaning softly in pleasure.

Lately she'd been noticing other things, pleasures that awakened her senses. Just this morning, she'd taken a good whiff of her bath gel and realized it smelled like raspberries. She'd picked it up haphazardly at the drugstore, never thinking much about the smell.

Then, she'd noticed how soft her new T-shirt was. It was something she'd never purchase for herself, pink with a picture of a kitten on it. But her aunt—the only blood relative Robyn still had contact with—had given it to her. Apparently she thought Robyn was still twelve years old. Robyn wore it because it was hanging in the closet and it was clean.

But it was also soft, a really soft cotton-silk blend.

It was as if her senses had been dead for years, and now they were waking up. Whether it was because she was doing something proactive to free Eldon from prison, or due to the man sitting across the table from her, she didn't know.

All she knew was that she normally picked at her food, and today she was well on her way to cleaning her plate.

"Good?" Ford asked.

She swallowed. "Amazingly." She ate several more bites, glancing up every once in a while to see Ford enjoying his carne asada—bits of thinly sliced steak, marinated, grilled and served with warm tortillas, grilled onions and guacamole.

He was certainly a man who appreciated good food. She idly wondered if his other senses were as highly attuned as his sense of taste. If his sense of touch, for instance, were properly aroused, would he wear that same, satisfied smile?

She made herself look away as blood rushed to her face and warmed other parts of her body, as well. Damn it, this was so wrong of her. Hadn't she, only a few hours earlier, counseled herself to bury her lust?

But some feelings were not so easy to ignore.

Slightly embarrassed by an appetite more appropriate for a football linebacker than an art teacher, she set her nearly empty plate to the side and took a sip of her tea.

"So," she said briskly, "how do we get this Roy guy to talk? Do we have to pay him?"

"It's a touchy subject. If we pay him, we have to disclose that fact. And it doesn't look good."

"But people pay confidential informants all the time, don't they?"

"The key word is confidential. They don't appear in court, they don't give depositions. They remain anonymous. Generally, they're used to help the police develop leads. The information they provide steers investigators in the right direction, but it doesn't become part of the evidence, per se."

"So you're saying, if we pay him he might provide some useful information, but then he wouldn't be able to testify in court."

"Right. The fact that we paid him would taint his information. If he testified to something that exonerated Eldon, it would look as if we had bribed him. Especially since his witness statement doesn't appear in the original police file."

"Maybe we should send Trina to talk to him. She's pretty persuasive. Honestly, you should hear her on the phone. She can turn those tears on and off at will."

Ford thought about it for a moment, taking another gulp of tea. "That's not a bad idea. But I was thinking *you* should talk to Roy."

"Me? Oh, yeah. I did so well with Heather."

"We both bombed out with Heather. But you're a beautiful woman, and Roy is a twentysomething man. He might respond to you."

Robyn felt her face heating again. "Beautiful, my ass," she mumbled, looking down at her worn jeans and her silly kitten T-shirt. She'd deliberately not worn much makeup today, only a bit of tinted moisturizer and clear lip gloss, because she'd been mortified at the possibility that Ford would think she was primping for him. "If you want beautiful, Trina is your woman."

"I'll admit Trina has a certain something. She's glamorous. Blatant. You, on the other hand—"

"Not glamorous. No one would accuse me of that."

"I was going to say, you have a deep down, natural beauty. Without the makeup and hair and sexy clothes, Trina would probably be quite ordinary. You, on the other hand…I'm sorry, am I making you uncomfortable?"

"Yes," she said without hesitation. She wasn't beautiful. She was slim, but not very shapely. One of her mom's boyfriends used to tease her that she had to wear her jeans real tight or they would slide right off. Her hair was straight, the color a plain, unadorned blond—not the platinum she'd sported in high school. She didn't frighten small children, but beautiful?

Ford had an angle.

"Sorry," he said, not sounding all that contrite. "I didn't mean to embarrass you. Do you ever date? Have you had a relationship since your divorce?"

"Why do you want to know?" she asked, not aggressively, but with genuine curiosity.

"I told you, I like to know who I'm working with. The more responsibility I give you, the more important it is for me to know you inside and out. So I'll know what to expect from you. So I can predict how you'll handle things."

"You think I should ask this Roy character on a date?"

"No. No, of course not." He shoved his plate aside, irritated. "You didn't answer my question."

"Do I have to?"

He shrugged. "It's your choice."

"No, I haven't had a serious relationship. When I lost Justin, I lost any capacity I had to love. That part of me died with him."

"I'm sorry." He sighed impatiently. "I spend a lot of time saying that to you, don't I?"

"You don't need to."

"If I cause you pain, I do."

"So, where did you say this Roy guy lives?" she asked, even though she already knew. They were in desperate need of a change of subject. "If you think I should talk to him, I will."

"I've offered to fly him here from Bozeman, or go see him there, but he's playing hard to get. I gotta work on him some more."

"Let me know if I can help. I'd enjoy a trip to Montana. Anything to get out of this heat." For the third day in a row, the temperature had topped a hundred degrees.

"Yeah, if I were Roy I wouldn't want to come here, either," Ford murmured.

Robyn made a quick decision. "I'll go to Montana. I'm probably of more use there than here, blindly calling wig shops and getting verbally abused."

Her decision seemed to energize Ford. "I'll make the reservations. We can probably get on a plane by this evening."

Robyn tried not to let her shock show on her face. "You're going with me?"

"Of course. I wouldn't let you face this guy alone. I'll get the local sheriff to help out, maybe loan us an interrogation room so anything Roy says is on the record."

Robyn could see the wisdom of that strategy. Still, when she'd volunteered to travel, she hadn't visualized taking the trip with Ford. Out of town. Away from prying eyes. In close quarters on a plane, then at a hotel.

But if she backed out now, Ford would want to know why. She couldn't tell him it was because she was starting not to trust herself alone with him.

CHAPTER EIGHT

DESPITE HIS OPTIMISM, Ford wasn't able to get a flight to Bozeman until the following afternoon. Though Robyn was impatient to go, she was grateful not to cancel her art class. Those kids kept her rooted in reality and reminded her that she had a purpose in life beyond freeing Eldon from prison.

The kids had all been so excited to see their finished ceramic projects, Arnie most of all. He'd gazed at the bright red vase, transfixed, then had smiled the biggest smile Robyn had ever seen.

"This is so cool! It's just so cool! When can I do another one?"

Some of the other boys made sucking noises, but Arnie ignored them. So did Robyn.

"I'm teaching a whole semester of ceramics in the fall. You can sign up for that. For the next couple of weeks, we're working on collages."

She showed the kids some examples of collages done by professional artists, including a few that were hanging in museums, to expand their imaginations beyond magazine pictures and construction paper. Just as she started passing out materials, someone knocked on the door.

She was surprised to see Ford standing there. "I thought we were meeting at the airport."

"I was working on something out this direction and I finished early," he said easily. "I thought we could ride to the airport together, save some gas and parking fees."

"We don't have to leave now, do we?" She looked at her watch. Had he booked an earlier flight?

"No, finish your class. I'll, um, watch."

The kids were quiet, listening intently. She shook her head at Ford. "Nobody in this class watches. We all participate. Right, kids?"

They razzed him a bit. She thought he would go somewhere else to kill time, but to her surprise, he agreed to make a collage. "This will do me good. I never took art in high school, remember." He found an empty seat at one of the large tables. It happened to be next to Arnie, who pointedly moved his chair farther away.

"Okay, then. You can all start going through the bins and find some things to inspire you." She had plastic tubs filled with all kinds of materials—paper, fabric, buttons, found objects, bits of old hardware, empty cans. "Anything can become art."

Robyn intended to do her own collage. She found it was often more effective to let the kids covertly watch and imitate her, rather than telling them what to do. She dived into the bins with abandon, gathering handfuls of fabric scraps, yarn and old buttons.

A picture took shape in her mind, a long-legged bird, maybe a heron.

Ford and Arnie were both sifting through contents in a bin next to hers. "Hey, I was gonna use that," Arnie said belligerently.

"My mistake," Ford said. "Here, you can use it."

Arnie tried to stare him down, but Ford could outstare anybody. "Nah, that's okay, you can have it," Arnie said. The object they were haggling over was an old light switch plate.

"Thanks," Ford said.

The class went pretty well after that, other than one screaming fit when a girl got glue in her hair. Instead of using the cardboard provided, Arnie started a 3-D collage on an upturned coffee can. He wasn't the best at following directions, but he showed a real flair.

Ford's collage was a disaster, but she could see he was throwing himself into it. Even more exciting was the fact that Arnie and Ford were talking, artist to artist, comparing their masterpieces, offering comments.

"You're hogging the glue," Arnie said, but without any anger. "You're using too much, that's why it's all goopy."

"Oh."

"Watch Ms. J, she just uses little drops."

"Like this?"

"Yeah. Now you got it, man."

Robyn bit her lip to keep from smiling too big.

Now Arnie had become not just an artist, but a teacher, with Ford his willing student. Some people were just full of surprises.

"ARE YOU AFRAID OF FLYING?" Ford asked. Their DC-9 wasn't even in the air yet, it was merely taxiing toward the runway, but Robyn had a white-knuckle grip on her armrests.

"I've never flown on a commercial airline before," she admitted.

"You're kidding. What about when you were married?"

"Anytime we flew, Eldon chartered a private Lear jet. Also, we never flew at night. And I didn't care for flying even then. But this is…I hadn't expected it to be so claustrophobic."

Ford placed his hand over one of hers. It was ice-cold. "You should have told me. I probably could have swung first class. Would you rather sit on the aisle?" He'd chosen the aisle for himself because his long legs didn't fit otherwise, and he ended up with his knees in his face. But he didn't want Robyn to be uncomfortable.

"No, I'd rather be here where I can look out the window."

Ford felt helpless. He had no brilliant ideas for instantly curing a phobia. Flying had never bothered him.

When the plane took off, he kept his eye on Robyn. She maintained her death grip on the armrests, and once when the plane hit turbulence, she even grabbed onto his arm. Her eyes were closed, her face tense.

"It'll smooth off once we get to a cruising altitude," he said. "The weather is supposed to be good all the way to Montana."

"Hope so."

At the first opportunity, he signaled the flight attendant. "As soon as possible, can we get a couple of drinks here? A bourbon on the rocks and, um…" He had no idea what Robyn would like, but he suspected if he asked her, she would say she wanted nothing. "How about a white wine?"

The flight attendant jotted down his order. "It'll be just a minute."

When the Fasten Seat Belts sign went off, the drinks appeared almost immediately. Ford paid, then pulled down both his tray table and Robyn's.

She opened her eyes and stared pointedly at the wine. "What's this?"

"It'll take the edge off."

"I don't normally drink."

"You did in high school."

She laughed, despite her obvious anxiety. "I did a lot of things in high school I would never do now. Once I made the decision to turn my life around, I quit the underage drinking. Never developed much of a taste for it after that, though Eldon tried to teach me to appreciate good wine."

"A little wine might ease your nerves, so you

don't spend the whole flight miserable. I can order something besides wine, if you prefer."

She looked at him, indecisive at first. "I'll take the wine, thanks," she finally said. She opened the tiny bottle and poured it into her plastic cup, then took a couple of healthy swallows. "Hmm. Not quite as good as the wine Eldon used to buy, but better than the screw-top sangria I drank in high school."

Ford reclined his seat the entire two inches that were allowed, then tasted his own drink. Not the best bourbon in the world, either.

"Did you drink in high school?" Robyn asked. "I remember seeing you at some of those wild bashes at Randy Baker's house."

"Not during football season," Ford said. "Other times, yeah, a little. Seems like liquor was everywhere back then. We all had fake IDs, or we raided the parents' liquor cabinets."

"Yeah, I didn't have to look far to find it."

Ford grimaced. He'd forgotten that Robyn's mother had been an alcoholic. He probably should have asked her before just plunking wine down in front of her. But she drank it, and when he asked her if she wanted another, she nodded.

"It's helping a little, I think."

"So, you were right about Arnie," he said, trying to distract her.

She looked at him quizzically. "How so?"

"He's got talent. Even I could see it. I thought he was just sucking up to you or manipulating you somehow. I was convinced a kid like him couldn't possibly be interested in art."

"A kid like him?" she asked, challenge in her voice.

"Yeah, you know. Juvenile delinquent. Gang-banger. Always in trouble. It was interesting, watching how absorbed he was in creating, how seriously he— What?" Her expression had thunder written all over it.

"It's the labels. Juvenile delinquent, gangbanger. Do you have any idea how harmful those labels are? Once a kid earns something like that, it's impossible for him to shake it off. Even if he wants to change. Even if he changes—"

"Robyn, whoa."

"Sorry, but that is one of my hot buttons."

"It's human nature to judge people by their past behaviors. If someone's an ax murderer, you still don't want to go out in the woods alone with them, even if they haven't killed for a couple years."

"So you're saying people can't change."

"I'm saying change is hard."

"Damn straight it is," she murmured. "You have no idea—the peer pressure, the lack of role models, the temptations. It's hell being a confused kid without everyone throwing labels at you."

She was referring to herself now. What labels had she been given in high school? *Druggie. Slacker. Thief.* Maybe even *slut.* Those labels were the very thing that made her forbidden fruit. Part of her allure, but labels nonetheless.

Ford tried again. "I was about to say, if you'd given me the chance, that Arnie busted those stereotypes wide open. He proved you were right about him, and I was wrong. You're making a positive change in his life, and you should be proud."

"We'll see if it sticks," Robyn said, but he could tell she was still not sure of him. "I'd like to find some way to keep him involved after the class ends. Sometimes the kids really respond, you know, but then they walk out of the class and never pick up a pencil or paintbrush again. Arnie wants his own pottery wheel, but they're so expensive. If I could buy him one, I would."

He could understand her identifying with the kid. Once she'd discovered her love for creating art, she must have been frustrated that she couldn't afford the art supplies she'd most likely wanted.

But frustrated enough to steal them? He was beginning to have serious doubts about what he and his fellow high-and-mighty tribunal members had done to Robyn.

"You really wanted to do that mural." He hadn't even realized he'd spoken aloud until she looked at him quizzically.

"What?"

"Arnie's situation made me think of yours. And the mural you designed. And how excited you must have been to win the competition."

"I was," she said, warily.

"Excited enough not to blow your chances by stealing a few dollars' worth of paints."

She raised one eyebrow. "So *now* you're thinking it through."

He sighed. "Maybe I owe you an apology."

"Maybe?"

"Just to set the record straight, it was your own art teacher who accused you. She was very passionate in her belief that you were the culprit."

"Yeah, Ms. Tanner was big on passion, short on facts."

"I can see that now."

"But you couldn't then? You were an honors student. Were you really that blind? Or were you paying me back because I rejected you?"

"That is not the case. I truly believed you were guilty. Ms. Tanner was an authority figure, and she was persuasive. It wasn't just me. All three of us voted guilty."

How had his apology turned her against him?

"I made the wrong decision," he said quietly. "But it was the best I could do at the time. I'm apologizing for it now. What more can I do?"

She gave him a little half smile. "That's all anyone can ask…that you do your best at any given time. I accept your apology, Ford."

He was relieved about that, at least. But he couldn't help feeling that he'd somehow lost an argument;

Robyn had been talking about more than just an isolated incident in high school.

BY THE TIME THEY TOUCHED DOWN in Bozeman, Robyn wasn't exactly relaxed, but she didn't look like she was about to face the gallows, either. They hadn't checked luggage, so they walked directly outside the small airport and hailed a cab.

"This cool night air feels divine," Robyn said, lifting her hair off her neck. "Nice place to have a summer house."

Ford watched her, blatantly enjoying the view of her tossing her head back, inhaling the rarified Montana summer night breeze. She was such a gorgeous creature, and she had no idea what she did to him.

By the time they arrived at their hotel—the nicest one he could find in Bozeman, because Daniel insisted his employees treat themselves well when they traveled on the job—Robyn finally seemed at ease.

He'd requested that Celeste book them a two-bedroom suite rather than two separate rooms so they would have a place to spread out and work on their strategy for facing Roy White. As they rode up in the elevator, though, he wondered if he'd made a mistake. Robyn looked way too enticing in her skinny black jeans and a clingy red shirt, her long hair mussed from running nervous fingers through it one too many times. Her sky-blue eyes seemed too big for her face.

God, he could drown in those eyes, just dive into

them and never surface. Knowing she would be sleeping in the next room, only a few steps away…

She folded her arms and drummed her fingers on her arm. "Slow elevator."

"Uh-huh."

"Nice hotel, though. You guys at Project Justice have it pretty good."

"Staying in nice hotels and getting a decent salary beats the hell out of working for the police department," Ford agreed. "Plus, Daniel doesn't ask his people to settle for less than he would. But I never worked as hard when I was a cop. Project Justice is pretty much a 24/7 job."

"Is that why you haven't remarried?" When he raised an eyebrow at her, she shrugged in feigned innocence. "Hey, you interrogated me about my love life. Don't you think it's fair I know more about who *I'm* working with?"

"I haven't had time to date, much less get married again. It wouldn't be fair."

"Not fair, how?"

"The job demands too much of me. There's not enough left to keep a wife or girlfriend happy."

"Once you're done with this case, you'll have all the time in the world. You are still planning to quit Project Justice, right?" The question sounded like a challenge.

"As soon as this case closes, one way or another."

"Probably for the best," she said as the elevator doors opened and she sauntered out ahead of him.

He followed, frowning. "What do you mean by that?"

"Just that, to work this job you have to have your heart and soul invested to do your best job."

"You don't think I'm invested enough in this case?" Try as he might not to care, her assessment bugged the hell out of him.

"Well, I did have to push pretty hard to get you to help me. You wouldn't be human if you didn't feel some resentment at being forced to do something you really didn't want to."

"You're right, I don't like being manipulated. It's just that once I got my teeth into the case, I forgot to be mad. I can't deny that I enjoy the work."

She stopped and turned suddenly, and he almost ran into her. "Then why quit?"

"Enjoying the work itself doesn't mean I can live with the results."

"You mean Katherine Hannigan."

Every muscle went tense at the mention of that name. He sidestepped Robyn and continued down the hall. "If you know what's good—for both of us— you'll drop the subject. Why would you even bring it up? It's distracting."

She hurried to catch up. "I'm sorry. See, you're not the only one who can be insensi— Oh, my God."

Oh, my God indeed. Ford had just opened the door to their suite. But it wasn't the standard two-bedroom suite he'd requested. This was clearly the bridal suite.

The room before them was an enormous bed-room, complete with a gauze-draped canopy bed and enough cabbage roses to give Laura Ashley night-mares. There was also a bottle of champagne chill-ing in an ice bucket and an enormous fresh flower arrangement.

"There had better be a second bedroom," he said as he stalked into the room and opened the first door he saw. It led into a palatial bathroom with a made-for-two Jacuzzi whirlpool bath, a shower big enough that the entire Dallas Cowboys team could get clean at the same time. Everything was pink-and-white—the tile, the sink, the piles of fluffy towels.

He rushed out and tried another door. Closet. Then he was out of doors.

"I know I had a couple of glasses of wine," Robyn said, "but I think I would remember if we got married."

He was glad she could maintain a sense of humor. He didn't think it was all that funny. He grabbed the phone and called the front desk. "There's been a mistake. I did not request the bridal suite...did I?"

A nasty suspicion occurred to him. He hadn't per-sonally made these reservations. Celeste had done it for him. Celeste was not in the slightest way incom-petent, nor was she senile, so he could only assume she had done this on purpose. Why, he had no idea. Sometimes her actions furthered her own agenda, but her motivations were often murky to everyone but herself.

"That's what I have written down," the front desk clerk said. "Bridal suite."

"Well, do you have something else? I'm on a business trip with a colleague, for God's sake."

The clerk hemmed and hawed a bit, but finally came up with a second room on the third floor.

"I'll take it," he said curtly. "Have someone bring up the key." He hung up to find Robyn grinning.

"Oh, come on. You've got to admit, it's a little bit funny. This room is over the top even if we were newlyweds. It's a nightmare only a ten-year-old girl could like."

Ford forced his tense shoulders to relax. He should be grateful she'd gotten past her pique with him and his labels. "A little bit funny. Let's get to work." He cleared the lace tablecloth and flower arrangement from the table for two, opened his briefcase and pulled out a folder of notes and a clean legal pad. For the next two hours, they worked on how they would approach Roy White.

Or rather, Ford tried to focus. But his gaze kept straying to Robyn's slender, expressive artist's hands. Whether she was gesturing animatedly or resting her hands on the table, Ford kept imagining them on his skin.

Then there was her mouth. Lipstick never seemed to last long on her lips, but it was the sexiest mouth he'd ever seen. When she was thinking hard, she had a tendency to worry her full lower lip with her front teeth.

Her perfume wasn't obvious, like Trina's, but every time they leaned close to look at something one of them had written, he smelled *something*. Shampoo, soap. The scent was sweet and clean and light.

That frilly bed was so, so close, and Robyn was slowly driving him crazy, though he was sure every provocative gesture she made was unconscious. She had said she was done with men, and he took her at her word.

Not that he would sleep with her under these circumstances. Under *any* circumstances.

When they were finally finished, it was close to eleven o'clock. Ford was torn between lingering, drawing out his time with her, and fleeing like his ass was on fire.

He opted for the ass-on-fire choice.

"I'll meet you in the restaurant around seven-thirty for breakfast," he said as he packed up his notes. "Then we'll head for the asphalt company where Roy works. Try to get some sleep."

"I will."

He didn't take a full, comfortable breath until he was on the elevator, heading for his own room.

ROBYN STARED AT THE CLOSED door, dismayed. The room seemed suddenly empty without Ford. He'd left so quickly, she hadn't had time to adjust to the idea.

Get some sleep. She didn't think that was possible. Though the wine should have left her tired and ready for bed, she was wound up so tightly she had a hard time breathing.

She loved working with Ford, and it went beyond simple relief that someone competent was on her side, fighting to free Eldon. She loved the way Ford's mind worked. When he brainstormed, ideas flowed out of him like a river. He made quick, logical connections, and sometimes she struggled to keep up with his train of thought barreling down the tracks.

She loved working with her students, of course, but it was a welcome distinction to stretch her intellect with an equal. More than an equal—he was brilliant. He'd been smart in high school, but she hadn't realized quite how deep his thoughts ran. In her own way, she'd labeled him: Smart, sexy-but-hollow jock.

He was anything but hollow.

It was easy to see why the work attracted him and why he so often succeeded, even though he didn't want to acknowledge his own skills right now.

Robyn changed quickly into pajamas, brushed her teeth, then climbed into the ridiculously huge bed, nearly twice as big as her bed at home. And twice as empty-feeling.

She hadn't realized how much she missed having an intimate connection with a man, someone to hold her in bed, someone to share ideas with, share a meal with.

Although she did not want Eldon ever again—Ford need not worry on that account—she suddenly missed some of the things she'd had with him, especially at first. She missed the domestic tranquility, the small things shared only between two intimates.

And yeah, the sex. She and Eldon had never made fireworks together, but even their tranquil couplings, the physical bond they'd forged had brought them closer, at least at first.

She suspected sex with Ford would be anything but tranquil. Not that she would ever find out. He seemed oblivious to her growing attraction to him.

Which was good. She was simply reacting to the stress, longing for reassurance. In a very short time, Eldon would either be free, or he would be dead, and she was sure her attraction to Ford would be dead, too.

CHAPTER NINE

ROY WHITE LOADED ASPHALT onto trucks for a living.
It was nasty, smelly, hard work, and he seemed more
than happy to take a break with his supervisor's
blessing when Ford and Robyn showed up to talk
to him.

They had decided not to ask the local police for
help. Given his criminal history, having cops around
might just stifle him.

Instead, the supervisor, who seemed impressed
with Ford's credentials and his current mission, provided them with a private office in the concrete-block
building that housed Hermann's Asphalt.

Roy was a short, stocky man, but powerfully built
with huge arm muscles and a thick neck. He had
black curly hair, long and bushy, kept off his face
with a green knit cap.

He smiled affably, seemed eager to help, until he
saw the tape recorder come out.

"I don't really like that recorder," he said. "Can
we turn it off?"

"We need an official record of this meeting," Ford
explained for the third time. "I could take notes, but

it wouldn't be nearly as compelling as your recorded voice."

"I don't know that much," he said, contradicting what he'd told Ford over the phone. "It's probably nothing."

"If it turns out that's true, then we won't use the tape," Ford argued sensibly.

Roy shrugged, grabbed a plastic office chair that was against the wall, swiveled it around and straddled it backward. "Okay. Let's get on with it."

Robyn settled in her chair, not liking Roy on sight, though she wasn't sure why. He was just a guy who was reluctant to get involved. Maybe it was the slightly salacious way he looked at her. Maybe it was because he didn't seem to care much whether some guy in Texas got fried or not.

Ford asked him a series of easy questions, starting with his name and age, where he'd lived at the time of Justin's disappearance, his job at the pizza restaurant, his hours. Once Roy got talking, he seemed to like the sound of his own voice, and he relaxed.

The questions got more specific, and so did the answers. Roy seemed to have an excellent memory of that long-ago day's events, including the exact time he'd gone on his break.

"How are you so sure about the time?" Ford asked, though in a friendly way. He was testing the waters, seeing how Roy would react to being pushed. If he provided a statement that supported Eldon's claims, the cops would grill him six ways to Sunday.

"I worked at that job for three years, same hours, and I always took my break at 12:15 a.m. A working man watches the clock. Although maybe y'all never had jobs where you worried about that kinda thing." He said it almost as a challenge.

Ford glanced at Robyn. Though she had remained almost completely silent during this interview, he expected her to say something now.

"I'm a teacher," Robyn said, not wanting to disappoint Ford. "I watch the clock plenty." But not because she looked forward to the end of her workday. A school ran on one-hour blocks of time, and she had to be cognizant of them.

Still, she hoped maybe the fact she worked for a living would build rapport with Roy, make him more sympathetic to her cause.

Roy turned his attention to her. "So you're married to this guy in prison?"

"I was at one time."

"And you're trying to get him off? Man, if I was on death row, my ex-old lady would laugh her ass off."

Robyn bristled, and Ford shot her another look. Though she wanted to argue, she knew she couldn't.

"Well, he is the father of my child," she said.

"Let's get back to that night," Ford said briskly. "You went on your break at 12:15 a.m. And what did you do?"

"I took a leak, then went out the back door to the

parking lot to have a smoke. A joint, actually." He smiled slyly. "Since you're not a cop, I can say that, right?"

Although Ford didn't visibly react to the statement, Robyn could almost feel the disappointment gnawing its way through him. Roy had been stoned when he saw whatever he saw. That was probably the reason the cops had discounted his statement. It wasn't just the "one beer" Robyn had originally thought.

Damn. This whole trip might have been for nothing.

Ford's next statement was deceptively casual. "Were you always stoned at work?"

"A lot. But it was just a couple of hits. Not like I was stumbling around or anything. You can't work around those hot pizza ovens if you're out of it."

"So what happened next?"

"I saw the dude drive up. I noticed the car. A Jag. I always notice cars."

"You're referring to Eldon Jasperson?"

"Yeah. I watched him get out. He seemed like he was in a hurry when he went inside."

"Could you see anyone else in the car?" Robyn asked, unable to stop herself.

But Roy shook his head. "Tinted windows."

"So is that it?"

"No. This is the important part. Just when I headed back inside, another car pulled into the parking lot."

Robyn sat up straighter. No one else had reported

seeing a second car. No other customers had arrived to pick up pizza.

"You told the police this that night?"

"Yeah, and they seemed interested."

"What kind of car was it?" Ford asked, not sounding excited, but Robyn noticed his body language. Leaning forward. Engaged. Alert. This could be something.

"I don't know," Roy said.

Robyn wanted to leap across the table and throttle the answer out of him. She literally sat on her hands to keep from reacting.

"You just said you notice cars."

"Yeah, but I was heading back inside. I was on to the next thing. I mean, if I'd known a murder was gonna happen, hell, I'd have taken pictures."

"Was it a big car? A small one? Do you know for sure it was a car, and not, say, a pickup truck?"

"I think it was a car," Roy said. "Not real big, not real small. Just, you know, average."

Robyn sighed inwardly. It was something, at least. Something to buoy Eldon's story that Justin had been snatched from his car. Whoever did it had to have arrived at the parking lot right about that time.

But a make, model and license plate might've been nice.

"What about the color?" Ford asked patiently. "Could you tell if it was light or dark?"

Roy thought about it. He really did seem to want to

help, though he'd been promised nothing, and Robyn had to respect him for that.

"I really don't remember."

Ford asked a few more questions, trying to elicit a memory, but nothing seemed to work. Finally, he admitted defeat and ended the interview. He turned off the tape recorder.

"So, did I help?" Roy asked. "You think the rich dude might want to reward me?"

Any positive feelings Robyn had been nurturing for Roy evaporated.

"This might help," Ford said. "I'll let Mr. Jasperson know you cooperated. He's a generous man."

"Guess that's good enough," Roy said glumly.

As soon as they were alone in the car, Robyn nearly exploded. "That's good, isn't it? That he saw a car? Even if he can't identify it, the fact that he saw any kind of car has to mean something, doesn't it? I mean, I know he was smoking pot—do you think that's why the police threw out his statement?"

"That would not be standard procedure. Even if you interview a falling-down-drunk witness who saw pink elephants robbing a bank, you write it down and include it in the report, along with your observation of the witness's impaired faculties. You don't throw it out."

"So, why do you think they threw it out?"

"Truthfully? I think within minutes of the cops showing up on the scene, in their minds they already had Eldon arrested, tried and convicted of the crime."

"I was a suspect for a while," Robyn said.

"Only briefly. Once they convinced themselves you weren't involved, Eldon was their man, and Roy White's statement didn't support their theory. So they made it go away."

"That's terrible."

"It happens more often than you'd guess. Cops coach witnesses, they plant evidence. Mostly because they are absolutely positive a certain person is guilty, and they're trying to ensure that person doesn't walk."

"Justice at any cost?"

Ford nodded. "I'm as guilty as anyone."

"You? I don't believe it. You would never plant evidence."

"No, but when I was a rookie, my overeager testimony put an innocent man behind bars." His voice was deceptively casual. But Robyn could see that the incident still affected him. His grip on the steering wheel tightened. "Years later, Project Justice got the sentence overturned."

"And you changed careers."

"Yeah. But it turns out I can do as much harm on the other side of the fence."

Katherine Hannigan again. She suspected that case was never far from his thoughts.

In a gesture that felt perfectly natural, Robyn placed her hand on Ford's arm. "Everybody does the best they can. You can't go through life believing you'll never make a mistake."

She expected him to close up. He had the last time this subject had come up. Instead, he sighed, as if giving in to her. "Yeah, but you can put yourself in a place where your mistakes don't spell life and death for other people."

"If everyone thought that way, we wouldn't have any doctors or lawyers or cops. Humans aren't perfect, and they never can be."

"There comes a time, Robyn, when the mistakes pile up and you have to take yourself out of the game. I only hope I don't add the Eldon Jasperson case to my list of failings."

"Ford. Even I know this is a long shot. If we can't save Eldon—" Her voice caught. She shouldn't be this emotional about her ex-husband. But she'd only recently come to terms with the fact that he might actually be executed.

She swallowed a couple of times. "If we can't save Eldon, as least we know we tried. It's all anyone can ask."

Ford placed his hand on hers. "Thank you."

ROBYN AND FORD SAID LITTLE during the flight home from Montana. Ford had spent most of the flight making notes to himself in a pad of paper he kept with him constantly. Robyn dozed.

She woke once, appalled that she'd been leaning her head on Ford's rock-hard shoulder. "Oh, sorry."

"It's okay," Ford said. "I'm glad you could sleep."

"Hmm, it is a little strange I'm not clinging to the ceiling." She was just too tired to be nervous.

"This flight has been a lot smoother than the last one. Feel free to nap some more, we're still an hour out. You can use me for a pillow anytime."

How about tonight? In her bed. She was so exhausted, she almost blurted her thoughts aloud. Spending so much time with Ford, feeling an attraction she couldn't act on, was taking its toll.

She suspected—no, she knew—that Ford felt something for her on a physical level. But even if they didn't have that disagreeable high school history hanging over them, he wouldn't act on his desire now. She was his client, and anything that happened between them would be a breach of ethics.

Ford was nothing if not a rule follower. He wouldn't cross that line, not easily.

But after she ceased to be his client? If he succeeded in freeing Eldon?

She let herself fantasize about that for all of five seconds. In bed, they might create fireworks. But she was afraid they would create fireworks elsewhere, too. They were too different. Yeah, he'd apologized, but how many years had it taken for him to see that he might have made a mistake?

One apology didn't mean he'd changed. He still saw everything in black and white, right and wrong. She, on the other hand, wanted to give everyone a second chance, the benefit of the doubt. She saw everything as positioned on an infinite spectrum. Shades of gray.

They would always be at odds.

She did doze some more, but she pointedly leaned her head against the window.

It was after dark by the time Ford pulled up to the curb in front of Robyn's apartment. They were both exhausted after what felt like the longest day in history.

"Do you want me to walk you to your front door?" Ford asked.

Lord, no. If she got the man within a hundred feet of her bed she'd be on him like a flea on a dog, never mind the fatigue.

"We're in Green Prairie, remember? With one notable exception, we don't have violent crime here."

He didn't look convinced, so she grabbed her purse and carry-on bag, which sat at her feet, and made a quick escape.

As she fitted her key into the lock and turned it, she waved to Ford, and his Crown Vic eased away from the curb.

A moment later, she had every reason to wish he'd walked her up after all. Something in her apartment felt strange. She reached for the light switch, but before she connected, a shape came flying at her, knocking her to the ground. Her purse went sailing. She tried to break her fall with her left hand and succeeded only in wrenching it as she fell hard onto her left elbow. Her attacker scrambled upright and tried to escape out the front door, but Robyn, mindlessly angry, lashed out with her legs and tripped him. He fell on top of her and they tousled for a few seconds before Robyn came to her senses and stopped struggling.

"Just get out," she said. "I won't stop you. There's no reason to hurt me. It's too dark and I can't identify—"

The intruder shoved Robyn and she hit her head on the tile floor. Technicolor fireworks exploded behind her eyes. The next thing she knew, the intruder was gone, leaving behind only the lingering smell of sweat and fear mixed with the strange, incongruent smell of coconut.

Robyn started to rise, but it was dark and everything was spinning. The only thing she could make out was her glowing cell phone, which had apparently spilled from her purse.

She grabbed it with her uninjured arm and dialed.

"Robyn?"

Just the sound of Ford's voice calmed her. "Yes, it's me. Someone was in my apartment."

"Holy hell," he muttered. "Are you okay?"

"I think so. He's gone now."

"I'm three minutes away. Lock the door until I get there, and stay on the phone."

She didn't think she could stand, but she didn't want to tell him that or he would be more alarmed than necessary. "Okay." Her voice trembled like a little girl's.

Robyn counted the seconds until she heard his footsteps coming up the walkway. "Robyn, it's me," he called out. "You can unlock the door now."

No need. She'd managed to nudge the door closed with her foot, but that was as far as she'd gotten.

Ford opened the door and flipped on the light, almost tripping over her in his haste to get inside the apartment.

"Whatever you do, don't trip," Robyn said. "This tile floor is deadly."

"Holy shit." He dropped to one knee and grabbed her cell phone and punched furiously at the keypad. "My friend's been attacked," he said, urgently, but in a steady, even voice. "I need an ambulance." He rattled off her address.

"Ford," Robyn objected. "That's not necessary."

"The hell it isn't." He returned his attention to the phone. "Look, I'm a former cop, and I know when an ambulance is needed. I'm capable of doing first aid without your coaching. Just send the paramedics." He set the phone down, but left the channel open. "Robyn, honey, where are you hurt?"

That's when Robyn saw all the blood. Her blood, soaking her clothes, smeared on the floor. Her universe shrank to the size of a pinhole. Distantly, she could hear Ford calling her name, but she couldn't seem to answer.

CHAPTER TEN

FORD HADN'T BEEN THIS SCARED since the night his partner had been shot. He'd walked the waiting room of another hospital that night, but this one looked the same. The hollow feeling in his gut felt the same, too.

Words couldn't describe how he'd felt when he saw Robyn on the floor and all that blood. If he ever found out who'd hurt her, he would strangle them with his bare hands.

"Ford?"

He looked up, surprised to see Raleigh standing next to him. "What are you doing here?"

"Daniel sent me. He said you sounded pretty upset on the phone. How is she?"

He sighed. "A cut on the back of her head, definite concussion, possible broken arm. She lost consciousness, but only for a few seconds, so I'm hoping it's not too serious. They're just checking her over."

"Oh. Oh, that's good. The way Daniel described it—"

"I overreacted." He'd been terrified, and he'd needed to tell someone. Daniel had seemed a good choice. He was the closest thing Ford had to a best friend, and he was a person who could cut through red tape and get things done.

He hadn't expected Daniel to send in reinforcement troops.

"You don't have to stay," he said, eyeing Raleigh curiously. She looked different tonight.

"I don't mind hanging around. A hospital waiting room is no place to be alone. And stop staring. You've never seen me out of my lawyer uniform, that's all."

He snapped his gaze away. No one would accuse Raleigh of being warm and fuzzy.

She was right, though. In all the time he'd worked with Raleigh, he'd never seen her wearing anything but those frumpy suits she favored and her flat, sensible shoes. Her armor.

Tonight she had on faded jeans, a clingy red T-shirt and scuffed cowboy boots. Her hair was damp, as if she'd just washed it, but it wasn't slicked back in her usual style. Instead, she'd braided it loosely and tied the end of the braid with a ribbon.

Any other woman, he'd have told her she looked nice. But Raleigh might misinterpret the comment, and he knew she did not respond well to even the mildest flirtation. So he let it drop.

"As long as you're here," he said instead, "I'll tell you about Roy White."

Over the next few minutes, he brought her up to speed on Roy's statement.

"It's not as much as I was hoping for," Ford said.

"No, but it's something." Raleigh was now fully in lawyer mode. "This statement proves what we suspected. The Green Prairie Police rushed to judgment. They destroyed exculpatory evidence because it didn't support the conclusion they'd already drawn—that Eldon was lying, that he'd killed his own son. Regardless of the merit of Roy's statement, the fact that it once existed, yet did not become part of the case file, could be enough to get the verdict overturned."

"Really?"

"We can sure try. Let's get back to Robyn. Do you think the assault on her is connected?"

The small surge of optimism he felt quickly dissipated when he was reminded of Robyn. "I feel sure it is. Green Prairie isn't exactly a hotbed of violent crime."

Which meant *he* was responsible for her injuries. He should have known she might be in danger. She was working—very publicly—to free her ex-husband from prison by proving he was innocent. The real murderer might feel threatened by her actions and try to put a stop to them.

"It would be convenient if the real murderer tipped his hand," Raleigh said.

"Not at the expense of more innocent people getting hurt."

"No, of course not. But if you're right, the killer is getting desperate. Did you call the police, by the way?"

"Yeah. They thought *I* was the one who assaulted

her. Bunch of yahoos." If Robyn hadn't regained consciousness just as they were about to put the cuffs on him, he'd be in jail right now.

"Do I need to step in?"

"No, it's straightened out. They're treating it as a run-of-the-mill break-in, and I don't feel inclined to correct them. Local cops would just muddy the waters."

Raleigh nodded, apparently agreeing with his statement.

A nurse walked into the waiting room, smiling in a place that didn't see many smiles. "Are you Ford?"

He jumped to his feet. "Yes. How is she?"

"You can see for yourself. Room two."

"I'm taking off," Raleigh said. "Have to be in court early in the morning."

"Thanks for coming."

"Hey, when Daniel says jump, I ask how high. But I would have come anyway," she added quickly. "Project Justice is the closest thing to family I have."

He hadn't known that about Raleigh. In fact, he didn't know personal details of anyone's life. He kept to himself, maybe too much. It felt a little strange, having Raleigh consider him part of her "family."

Robyn smiled brightly when he entered her treatment room. She was pale and had bandages around her head and her left wrist and hand. An IV pumped something into her arm. Otherwise, though, she looked pretty good. No blood, anyway.

He couldn't help himself. He reached her gurney in

two long strides and gathered her into a hug, a gentle one. "You scared the life out of me, woman."

"I'm okay, really, Ford. No broken bones."

He didn't want to let her go, especially because she was hugging him back with her uninjured arm. She felt so good, warm and alive. Her hair was damp against his cheek and smelled of hospital soap.

"There was so much blood," he said.

"All from one small cut in my scalp. The doctor took four stitches. Now I have a bald patch."

"But you were unconscious. Don't you have a concussion?" He pulled back to study her eyes. They looked normal; the pupils were the same size.

"I have a mild concussion," she confirmed, "and a sprained wrist. That's it."

He forced himself to let her go. "I'm so sorry, Robyn. I should have known you might be in danger."

She smiled again. "Hey, you offered to walk me to the door. I'm the one turned you down."

"I should have insisted—"

"Ford. You can't take responsibility for every bad thing that happens around you."

"I'm not leaving you alone again," he declared. "Not until this thing with Eldon is settled. If some maniac is out there trying to kill you—"

"No, no, Ford, you've got it wrong. This can't be related to the case. The person who attacked me was really small—had to be a kid. He probably broke in looking for something he could pawn for drugs."

"Are you sure?"

"He fell on top of me, and he wasn't that heavy. This definitely wasn't someone out to kill me, or they'd have done a better job. He was just trying to get out, and I was in the way."

Ford wanted to take comfort in her explanation. But it seemed like such a coincidence for Robyn to become a crime victim at this particular time in her life. He didn't trust coincidence.

"Stop worrying," she said sternly. "No way the kid could have been involved in Justin's disappearance. He'd have probably been in grammar school at the time."

"Maybe there's no connection. But you could be in danger. We're going to be more careful from now on."

She reached up and lightly caressed his cheek. "Thank you for caring."

He realized he did care, far more than was advisable. How had this woman gotten under his skin?

Hell, he knew the answer. She'd been there since high school. But the girl on whom he'd had a silent, hopeless crush had matured into a smart, compassionate woman, the only woman he'd contemplated a relationship with since his divorce.

Not that she'd even consider it. She'd accepted his apology. But what he did to her in high school would always be between them.

A doctor walked in—young, Hispanic, not very authoritative or doctorly, which didn't fill Ford with confidence. The doctor nodded to Ford, but spoke to Robyn. "How are you feeling, Ms. Jasperson?"

"Fine, since you gave me those nice pain meds."

Ah. That might explain why she seemed so cheerful, holding on to his hand as if he was a boyfriend instead of a… What was he to Robyn, anyway? More than a colleague, it seemed. She'd called on him to help her in a crisis, rather than dialing 911, which would have been the sane thing to do.

"I'm going to let you go home," the doctor said. "But you have a concussion. Is there someone who can wake you up once every hour?"

Robyn frowned. "Umm, I guess I could go to—"

"I'll do it." Ford was the logical choice.

"You don't have to do that." She looked up at him, her blue eyes even bigger than usual.

He felt an almost irresistible urge to kiss her. "Yes, I do. You'll go home with me. My building has better security than yours." She opened her mouth to argue, but he didn't let her. "I'm not giving you a choice in this. I can't work to free Eldon and worry about you, too."

She looked at him mutinously for a couple of seconds, then caved. "Okay."

He suspected if she weren't high on pain meds, she would have argued more.

The fact she was drugged up was a good thing, he decided. No matter how tempted he was to claim her, he wouldn't, not when she was injured and without all of her faculties. He couldn't take advantage of her that way.

Maybe by the time she'd recovered, the temptation to do something utterly stupid would have passed.

ROBYN COULDN'T BELIEVE she'd agreed to stay at Ford's. She should have argued that she would be fine. But the codeine had muddled her thinking, and she'd found herself nodding and agreeing to whatever he suggested.

A few minutes later, her discharge papers and a prescription in hand, Robyn let herself be helped into the passenger seat of Ford's car.

She had to admit, she felt safer with him at her side. Despite her bravado, the assault had shaken her. She hadn't felt this vulnerable since she'd been a kid. Back then, one of her mother's boyfriends had hit her, and her mom, who was supposed to protect her, had done nothing to stop it.

"Do you want to stop at the drugstore and get that scrip filled?" he asked.

"I don't think so." She didn't like the fuzzy thinking, and the pain wasn't that bad. "If you have some Tylenol, that will do."

"I do."

"Where do you live, anyway?" she asked.

"Not far from the Project Justice offices. Daniel owns an apartment building downtown. He encourages his employees to live there. It's roomy and comfortable enough, and the rent is reasonable."

She was more than curious to see what kind of space Ford occupied. Would it be spartan, with only the bare minimum needed to survive? Or would it be a messy bachelor pad, crammed with junk?

"Did your wife live there when you were married?" She was appalled by her own question, but her usual polite reserve had deserted her, along with any manners, apparently.

He didn't seem to mind the question. "Nah, I lived on the city fringe when I was married. Suburbia, though it was still within the Houston city limits. Nasty commute."

"I have a hard time picturing you in suburbia."

"I did, too, apparently. We had the ugliest lawn on the block, a field of weeds surrounded by the neighbors' carpets of emerald-green velvet. Apparently, a suburban husband's first priority is healthy grass. One of many ways I did not measure up."

It made Robyn sad to think of some woman failing to appreciate Ford's good points. She had a feeling he would protect and cherish any woman he claimed as his own. He would be honest and steadfast, and she doubted he would cheat like her husband had.

She couldn't see Ford fertilizing lawns and firing up the grill on weekends. He seemed too serious for that mundane, domestic stuff. Then again, he'd made a collage in her art class, so obviously he made some room in his life for things other than work.

Did he make time for women? For sex?

She couldn't help smiling.

"What?"

"Nothing," she said, schooling her face into a frown. Those pain pills sure did some strange things to her brain.

Once they were downtown, Ford pulled into an underground garage that required a passkey for entry. Robyn hadn't realized they'd reached their destination; she craned her neck just in time to get a vague impression of his building. It was one of those funky old warehouses converted to apartments.

It was only when they were on the elevator that Robyn realized she had nothing but the clothes on her back—hospital scrubs, because she'd bled all over the clothes she'd been wearing. No telling what had become of those clothes; she'd been too out of it to ask.

She didn't have pajamas or a toothbrush, or clean underwear for the next day. With her hand swollen and wrapped in an elastic bandage, she didn't think she'd be up to hand-washing anything in the sink, even if she could stand up for that long.

Her concerns about personal hygiene faded to the background, however, when she got her first look at Ford's apartment.

Roomy was a vast understatement. It was huge. A carved oak front door led from the hallway to a marbled entry flanked by fat Doric columns. A crystal chandelier hung from the tall ceiling. Two steps down, and she was in a sunken living room the size of an Olympic swimming pool. The white carpeting seemed wildly impractical, and the red-and-black leather furniture, startlingly chic, just didn't look like Ford at all.

"Wow."

"I had nothing to do with the decor. The place came like this. Since my ex kept all our furniture, I snapped up the opportunity to live here."

"Who lived here before?"

"Some cousin of Daniel's. A model, I think. She hooked up with some Hollywood guy. I'll give you a tour tomorrow. Right now, it's almost midnight and we're both exhausted. Let's try to get some sleep."

Robyn allowed herself to be led down a hallway to the guest room. To her disappointment, the furnishings here were quite ordinary. Nice, but basic.

On the bed, made up with a striped comforter, she saw something that puzzled her—a small plastic bag of new toiletries, a set of blue cotton pajamas and some clean clothes, including under-things.

"What's all this?"

"I see Jillian's been here. She's Daniel's ever-efficient administrative assistant. I filled him in on our plans during the drive."

"You mean just now?"

"You were asleep."

She sighed. "I don't even remember falling asleep. Are you sure?"

"Unless you snore when you're awake."

She opened her mouth in mock umbrage. "I do not snore." But her mental state worried her.

"You've got a concussion," he said, more serious now. "It's normal to experience some confusion, even amnesia about the events just before the injury."

"Oh, I remember those just fine." If she closed her eyes, they came back to her in vivid detail—the sensation of the dark-clad form rushing toward her, getting knocked to the ground, the smells of fear and blood and coconut.

"Try to rest, okay? There's Tylenol in the medicine cabinet in your bathroom, if you need it. I'll wake you in an hour, but then you can go right back to sleep."

She nodded. "Ford…"

He stopped and looked at her questioningly.

Though it wasn't the wisest thing, she threw her arms around his neck for the second time that night. "Thank you. Thank you for coming to my rescue and taking care of me. Thank you for worrying about me. No one has worried about me in a long time."

"Then it's about time someone did." His voice was husky, and when she pulled back to look into his eyes, she saw something there, the hint of a hunger that matched her own.

Their faces were close, and for a moment, she thought he was going to kiss her again. She wouldn't have minded.

In the end, though, he tipped her head down and kissed her on the forehead.

"You're an amazing woman, Robyn. Good night."

Robyn felt like helium balloons were attached to

her as she brushed her teeth, washed her face, donned the soft pajamas and climbed into bed. Maybe it was the drugs, or maybe it was the way Ford had looked at her, like he wanted to cherish her and devour her all in one breath.

As she lay in bed with the soft, clean sheets cocooning her, she tried to hold on to that lovely memory. But she fell asleep almost instantly.

WHEN FORD'S PHONE BEEPED its alarm at him, he came immediately awake. It was time to wake Robyn. It seemed he'd just gotten into bed, but an hour must have passed.

He climbed out of bed and headed for his bedroom door, then realized he was naked. He found a pair of jeans and pulled them on.

Her door was open a crack. He tapped softly on the door. "Robyn?"

No answer, so he pushed inside. Her sleeping form was barely visible in the half-light drifting in from the window. Blond hair surrounded her head like it was blowing in the wind.

She was breathing, that much he could see. He hated to wake her when she looked so peaceful, but he had to.

He grasped her shoulder and squeezed. "Robyn?"
No response.

He shook her slightly and spoke louder. "Robyn?"
Suddenly her eyes flew open, filled with fear and

rage, and the next thing Ford knew, her right fist was speeding toward his face. He ducked out of the way, but she still managed a glancing blow to his chin.

"Robyn, wake up! It's okay. You're safe. It's me, Ford." He managed to trap her flailing arms before she hurt him or herself.

The light of reason gradually returned to her eyes, and she stopped struggling. "Oh, my God."

"You okay? Bad dream?" He let go of her wrists.

"Wow. Very bad dream. They were executing Eldon, except then they decided to execute me, too. There was this prison guard and an evil doctor trying to grab me so they could put the needle in my arm—"

She looked so frightened, so vulnerable, and Ford couldn't stand it. He gathered her up and held her against him. "It's okay, Robyn. You're safe. It was just a dream."

"I don't usually have nightmares. I certainly don't wake up screaming."

"You didn't scream."

She pulled back slightly to examine his face, running her uninjured hand along his stubbly chin. "I hit you. Ford, I'm so sorry."

"Nothing…to apologize for." Oh, hell. He had to get out of here. The way she was looking at him, the way she smelled, and they were practically in bed together.

Why couldn't he let her go? And why hadn't he taken the time to put on a shirt?

"I have to ask you some questions." He tried to sound businesslike, but couldn't pull it off. His voice was hoarse with desire, his mouth dry like that of a man stranded in the desert, and here was his drink of water.

"Questions?"

"Uh…" He couldn't think. "What's your name?"

"Oh, those questions. To be sure I haven't gone out of my head."

"Could you just answer, please?"

"Ernestine Grimdiddy."

"Robyn, behave."

She tucked her head against his neck. "If I answer the questions, will you stay with me?"

"I can't."

"I'd feel safer."

"You…" His voice felt gravelly and he cleared his throat. "You definitely wouldn't be."

They both let that reality linger in the air a few moments.

"What's your name?" he asked again.

She ran her hand down his bare chest and turned her head slightly, pressing her lips close to his neck. "Robyn Knotley."

He was about to come unglued. "That's your maiden name," he pointed out.

"Because I don't want to think about Eldon. Not anymore tonight, please. Tonight I need you, Ford."

He was strong, but not that strong. He had Robyn warm and pliant in his arms, kissing his neck… "What's your address?"

"The White House," she murmured as her lips traced a trail of fire up his neck toward his ear.

"What's today's date?"

"May 24, 1997."

"Do you want me to take you back to the hospital? Because I think you've lost your mind."

"Insanity's gotten a bad rap. It's a nice place to be." She nibbled his earlobe.

"Robyn." He grasped her chin and forced her to stop kissing him and look him in the eye. "You are on pain meds. I can't take advantage of that." No matter how much he wanted to.

The look she gave him was utterly sane. "The codeine has worn off. My name is Robyn Knotley Jasperson. I live at 305 Oak Bend Way, Apartment 6D. Today is July 13th. And I want you to make love to me, Ford Hyatt. No promises, no commitments, just you and me in this bed, tonight. I'll give you one chance to say no, and we won't speak of it again."

She dropped her hands and cast her eyes down.

"Liar," he muttered. "I don't have a chance in hell of walking away from this." With that, he pushed her down onto the pillows and did what he'd been thinking about for hours—kissed her in a way that she would know he meant business. This was no soft, lingering, gentle kiss, but a kiss of possession.

Maybe tomorrow, this night would be relegated to an unwise decision, a temporary interlude or a moment of insanity. But tonight, she was his.

CHAPTER ELEVEN

ROBYN'S HEAD HURT AND her wrist throbbed, a sure
sign that the drugs really had worn off. But once Ford
kissed her, new sensations washed the pain into the
background of her consciousness.

He wasn't taking advantage of her. If anything, her
deliberate seduction was a clear case of her taking
advantage of him—of his kindness, his concern, his
hospitality, not to mention his half-naked body.

For *that,* he had to accept some responsibility.
She maybe could have resisted if he hadn't walked
in here wearing only a pair of jeans riding so low on
his hips she knew he wasn't wearing underwear.

She drank in the kiss, surrendered to it. Yes, yes,
this is what she wanted, to lose herself in him, for
just a few minutes or an hour or a night.

She moaned low when he shoved his hand under
the hem of her pajama shirt. They were bland, sexless
pajamas, but suddenly she felt like the most desir-
able siren in the world. His hand reached her breast
and claimed it, surrounded it. He rubbed his callused
palm against the sensitive nipple until she moaned
again, sounding almost strangled.

"Want…naked," she managed to whisper when

he stopped kissing her long enough that she could gasp in a few breaths. She tried to work at one of the buttons on her top, but her left hand was useless in the bandage.

"I'll take care of that."

He did, kissing each inch of bare flesh that he exposed as he flicked the buttons open one by one, then spread open the edges, revealing her breasts to his hungry gaze.

He lowered his mouth to her left nipple, and she squirmed in delight as heat shot through her whole body and pooled between her legs.

She wasn't exactly inexperienced. Before Eldon she'd had a few boyfriends, and her physical relationship with Eldon had been perfectly adequate, even satisfactory at the time. But nothing in her past had prepared her for what she felt right now.

She wanted to tear at her clothes, at his, but now that he'd fallen in with her wishes, he'd taken utter command. Their coupling would proceed according to his timetable, and in her injured state, she wasn't in any shape to wrestle with him.

He didn't waste a lot of time, though; apparently he was in something of a hurry, too. He shoved his hands inside the elastic waist and cupped her bottom, his fingers barely teasing the tender flesh between her legs.

The more she tried to wiggle, the more firmly he held her, until finally he whisked the pajamas off in one deft movement, over her hips, down her legs and off.

He moved his hands back to her hips, his fingers finding the patch she wore just below her bikini line.

"Is this what I think it is?"

"Yes." She wore it to regulate her hormones. Fortunately, it worked as birth control, too. Ford might think she had lied about her nonexistent love life, but she would explain later, when she could string words together.

"Good," was all he said as he shucked his jeans.

Her breath caught when she saw him for the first time completely naked. He was gorgeous, fully aroused. The sight of him made her bones melt.

Ford returned his attentions to her, covering her body with his, allowing their naked skin to touch from shoulder to foot. His erection pressed against her belly, pulsing with desire. His skin was hot, his muscles hard, his belly firm, and she reveled in every sensation his nearness brought.

His hands roamed everywhere, hot and demanding, tracing every contour of her body as if trying to memorize her.

She was almost afraid to touch him, she was still so shocked that he was here, naked in her bed. What if he was a dream? What if he disappeared like a puff of smoke, and she discovered he'd been a figment of her addled brain?

But touch him she did, and he felt more real than

the bed beneath her. She smoothed her palms over the hard muscles of his back, down to his buttocks and back up again, gratified that he responded to her touch. He issued a feral growl whenever her hands strayed to those places daylight never touched.

"I can't wait anymore," he said. "I need to be—"

"Don't...want to wait." She parted her legs, inviting him to enter her.

The first touch of his erection against her body made her gasp with pure anticipation. He moved slowly, giving her body time to accommodate him. But though it had been a long time for her, she didn't want or need slow. She raised her hips off the bed, sheathing him more deeply inside her.

With a groan he thrust himself the rest of the way in, and for the first time in a very long time, she felt full. Physically, emotionally so full of Ford that she couldn't think of anything else.

They moved together in perfect harmony, as if they'd been making love for a decade. Though she wanted it all, now, he forced her to slow down and savor each sensation, drawing out each stroke deliciously. He might have been anxious to be inside her, but they lingered over their act of love.

This might be their only time together.

Robyn pushed that thought out of her mind. The past, the future had no place in this bed. There was only now, and she was determined to enjoy every last piece of Ford that he was willing to give her.

Ford's strokes came faster, more insistent, until

he was breathing hard with the exertion. A strange feeling came over Robyn, a delightful pressure building until she felt so filled with pleasure and joy she wanted to explode with it.

And then she did, the release so powerful she felt as if her pleasure filled the bed, the room, the whole universe.

Her climax reached a threshold and then remained there, giving her wave after wave of sensation, like nothing she'd imagined could exist in the world.

Ford gave one final thrust and his whole body tensed. Robyn forced her eyes open because she wanted to watch him. She wanted to remember his face in the throes of his own peak.

To her surprise he opened his eyes and looked right at her. Their gazes locked, and for one long, beautiful moment they were one.

His body spent, Ford finally broke the gaze and all but collapsed against her.

She put her arms around him, stroking his short hair with the fingertips of her uninjured hand. She wanted to say something, to tell him how happy he'd made her, but she was afraid words would trivialize the experience, so she remained silent, breathing in concert with him.

Ford shifted his weight to the side and their bodies parted. But he slid his arm beneath her and pulled her against his chest. "Is it okay like this?" he asked. "Am I hurting you?"

"No, feels nice."

"That was kind of rough. I should have been gentler, but I sort of forgot you were injured. I sort of forgot everything, including my name and what planet I was on."

She smiled and reached up to caress his face. "I felt no pain."

"This wasn't the best decision I've ever made."

"Shh. I don't want to hear it. Not now. Tomorrow, you can tell me all about what a terrible mistake it was, and I promise not to argue. But tonight, Ford Hyatt, you are mine."

He sighed, sounding relieved. "Deal."

They both went silent for a while, but Robyn could tell he wasn't sleeping.

"Hell," he finally said.

"What?"

"I still have to wake you up every hour. My phone's in the other room. It's what I use for an alarm."

Hell was right. If he got out of bed, he might not come back. Robyn made herself sit up and turn on the light. She'd seen…yes, there it was. An alarm clock on the nightstand. She set it to ring in an hour, then turned off the light and snuggled back against him.

"There."

When the alarm went off, it woke Robyn from the midst of a sexy dream. As she reached over blindly to silence the annoying alarm, she realized it wasn't a dream. Ford was lightly caressing the inside of her thigh.

"Mmm, that's a nice way to wake up," she said.

"I thought it was a particularly annoying buzz."

"Not the clock. This." She touched the back of his hand, then reached across her body to his and discovered he was as hard as a two-by-four.

"Oh, sorry."

"Sorry? You gotta be kidding." She ran her hand along the length of him, then swung one leg over him and pressed her breasts against his chest, letting the light, springy hair there abrade her nipples.

"Whoa."

Before he could lodge any more objections, she kissed him, long and low and lingering. "Ready for another round?"

"Oh, yeah. Wait a minute. What's your name?"

"I don't remember." She trailed a row of kisses along his jaw and down to his neck.

"Uh, what's your address?"

"Hollywood and Vine."

"What's…oh, hell, I can't remember the question. What's the date?"

"Bastille Day."

"Good enough for me."

FORD GOT LITTLE SLEEP that night, but he didn't care. Watching over Robyn while she slept in his arms was worth missing a few z's. Plus, they made love three times.

When the sun came up, he eased himself out of bed but let Robyn sleep. He wanted to stay there with her. Stay there all day, shutting out the rest of the world.

But as unwise as last night's decision to bed her had been, lingering over the sex would just heap on more stupidity. He wouldn't undo what he'd done for anything. Last night was an experience he would take with him to his grave even if he lived to be a hundred years old.

But now they had a job to do. He had to put his desires for Robyn out of his mind. That meant he had to put some distance between him and her naked body.

By the time he finished with his shower, he could hear running water in the guest room. Good, he wouldn't have to wake her. He shaved, dressed with a little more care than usual, and went to the kitchen to make breakfast. Eggs, toast, fruit, yogurt. He and Robyn both needed to replenish their energy reserves, and he intended to make her eat a good breakfast.

He was just taking the eggs out of the frying pan when Robyn entered the kitchen. Though he tried to steel himself from reacting to the sight of her, his heart still flipped over. She was wearing the velour workout clothes Jillian had left for her. They clung to the curves of her body in a way that made his mouth go dry. But her makeup-free face and the tousled tumble of her hair made her look young and vulnerable, too.

"Good morning," she said tentatively.

"Yeah, it is. You didn't get your stitches wet, did

you?" Probably not the most romantic thing he could have said. But they needed to transition away from romantic and back to businesslike.

"Um, no. I didn't get my head wet. I'll need help wrapping my wrist, but that'll keep till after breakfast. You cook?"

"Just scrambled eggs and toast. I believe in a good breakfast. If I ever make any other meal for you, it's likely to be sandwiches. Hope you're hungry."

"Starving, actually. I can't remember when I've been so hungry."

Good, he wouldn't have to force-feed her.

"What's on the agenda today?" She picked up their two plates from the counter and carried them to his kitchen table, a white, glass-topped modern thing as impractical as all the other furniture.

"First, we go to your apartment and pick up anything you'll need for the next couple of days. You can either stay in my guest room, or you can stay at Daniel's estate."

"That's not necessary. I'm sure whoever broke in won't be back."

"Yeah, well, I'm not. Every minute I spend worrying about your welfare is a minute I can't devote to proving Eldon's innocence. There's coffee. Help yourself."

She sighed as she poured herself some coffee, managing well with just one hand. "You're being unreasonable. I have classes to teach."

"It's Saturday. Your next class isn't until Tuesday.

When the time comes, I can drive you. Or if I can't, Daniel will provide a driver."

"That's ridiculous."

He brought a bottle of orange juice and two cartons of yogurt to the table. "Maybe, but that's how it's gonna be."

"Tyrant," she muttered as she set her steaming mug on the table. "If you weren't feeding me this lovely breakfast, I'd be pissed off."

He was pleased to see Robyn eating without prompting for a change. Two eggs, two pieces of toast, a glass of juice and at least some of the yogurt disappeared. He cleaned his own plate and struggled to keep his mind on work rather than letting his gaze stray to the intriguing shadow between her breasts, barely peeking out above the front zipper of her velour top.

"What next?" she asked as she drained her second cup of coffee.

"Let's go to your place. Maybe your intruder left some evidence. At least we can make sure the apartment is secure and you can grab whatever you need."

"Okay." She took their dishes to the dishwasher. "I'll need to change clothes anyway. Velour is nice in your air-conditioned apartment, but wildly impractical for triple-digit temperatures."

He put away the leftovers and turned off the coffee. "Do we need to talk about last night?" he asked suddenly.

"Not unless you want to." Her reply was light, almost indifferent. And he didn't buy it for a minute.

"I feel like I should apologize."

"Definitely not necessary." She closed the dishwasher and turned to face him. "We both wanted it. We both needed it. It kind of cleared the air, don't you think?"

"Not exactly." It wasn't as if he didn't want her as sharply as ever. Except it was worse, because now he knew what it was like to be inside of her, to hear the soft moans she made in the throes of pleasure, to feel the soft skin of her breasts.

He was at a loss. Conversations like these were one of the things that drove him and Kathy apart. He was supposed to guess what was going on in her head, and if he guessed wrong, it meant he didn't care.

Maybe it wasn't fair to compare Robyn with Kathy. The two women were nothing alike. But he still had no idea what was going on inside Robyn's head.

"If you were mad, you'd tell me, right?"

"Ford, of course. I'm not mad. If I had to wake up every hour and endure twenty questions, that was a helluva way to make it more pleasant."

Pleasant? Talk about understatement. How about mind-blowing?

But it would be stupid—even more stupid—to dwell on it. Not when the experience was never to be repeated.

ROBYN SWALLOWED BACK tears a dozen times on the drive to Green Prairie. Ford made small talk, and she responded appropriately, she thought. But his businesslike attitude confused her.

She wasn't angry. She hadn't lied about that. But she was hurt. She'd thought last night they had crossed a threshold, that they would be closer now. Crazy as it seemed, she'd even dared to believe they could have a future. Maybe not the white-picket-fence forever kind of future, but at least a future where they'd be closer than they'd been before.

She hadn't realized how much she'd missed physical intimacy. Sharing something with one other human being that no one else could understand. Making love with Ford had worked like a soothing balm on her battered soul, and she wanted more.

Apparently she wasn't going to get more. Ford viewed last night as a mistake, a lapse in judgment, something to apologize for. And she had no choice but to go along. It would be futile to chase him or long for something that could never be.

He had warned her, after all, that making love was against his better judgment.

When they reached her apartment, it took Ford only a few minutes to figure out how the intruder had gained access. He'd broken a small bathroom window and squeezed through.

A neighbor, or maybe the manager, had been kind enough to nail a couple of boards over the broken pane, so it wouldn't be easy for someone else to break in.

"You weren't kidding your attacker was small.

A grown man would have a hard time squeezing through that hole," Ford observed.

"So it almost had to be a teenager," Robyn said. "See? Probably not related to our investigation at all."

"Teenagers can be hired," Ford pointed out. "Until we know otherwise, we're going to treat this as if someone was trying to hurt you."

Robyn didn't argue because it was like a sheep bleating at a solid wood fence, expecting it to open.

She quickly changed into a cool cotton blouse and one of her more decent pairs of jeans, then gathered up the few things she would need—some more clothes and toiletries. She watered the wilted plants on her balcony, threw away some sad-looking tomatoes and half a head of lettuce, and gathered up the trash to take to the Dumpster so she wouldn't end up with ants, or worse, those giant flying cockroaches that loved the Houston climate so much.

The last stop she made was the mail room. A large, padded envelope had been stuffed into her box. She was puzzled by the return address, until she remembered about the wig shop receipts. Pleased that the shop owner had acted so quickly, Robyn tucked the package under her arm, sifted through the rest of the mail—all junk, which she tossed in the recycle can—and eagerly opened the padded envelope.

There were about a dozen receipts enclosed. Her heart beating wildly, she sifted through them quickly, noting the names: Vera Stearns, Chloe Bellflower,

Amos Jones—Amos Jones? Well, maybe he was buying a wig for his wife.

Conscious that Ford would be waiting for her, she ran out to the parking lot, where she'd spied Ford's car. She threw everything into the backseat except the handful of receipts and climbed in.

"What's that?" he asked.

"Wig shop receipts. I accidentally had them sent to my home address." She reviewed more names— Cynthia Ludlow, Bella Orizaba, Jasmine Tyson. None of the names…wait. Bella Orizaba…

"You got something?" Ford asked.

"Not really. It's just that name Bella Orizaba sounds kind of familiar to me. But I can't quite place it."

"We'll have someone check it out."

Deflated that she hadn't immediately found a clue to the wig buyer, she quickly flipped through the rest of the receipts, then shoved them back in the envelope. "I guess I was just hoping for a lightbulb to suddenly go off. You know?"

"Don't lose hope, Robyn. The receipts were a long shot, but we've got more to go on now. Raleigh said that Roy's statement might actually be useful in overturning the verdict."

"Really?"

"Possibly."

She could tell he didn't want her to get her hopes up, so she tempered her newfound optimism. "So, what now?" she asked brightly.

"We're meeting Raleigh and Daniel. I'm going to present what evidence we have to Daniel and see where we stand."

Uneasiness bloomed in Robyn's chest. She'd never met the man, but she knew Daniel Logan was the ultimate decision-maker. He had authorized Ford to take on Eldon's case, and he could just as easily un-authorize it if he thought it was a waste of time.

"So, I finally get to meet the mysterious Daniel. What's he like?"

Ford actually smiled. "You'll see."

"IT'S NOT ENOUGH," Daniel said. He was stretched out on a foam raft in his ridiculously huge swimming pool, sipping some fruity drink with a paper umbrella and doing something with his high-tech phone.

Ford sat perched on a cedar deck chair near the edge of the pool. Robyn and Raleigh were nearby, sitting at a table with an umbrella. At eleven o'clock in the morning, the heat was already punishing.

Daniel did this kind of thing all the time. Anyone who wanted a piece of his time had to take it on Daniel's terms, usually on his turf. He seldom left his estate, and why would he? He had everything here any man could want—swimming pool, horses and a practice polo field, tennis courts, and a lot of people he paid to keep things humming along.

The one thing Daniel did not have was a woman. Although something of a playboy before his arrest, he had not been romantically attached to a woman since. If he had any kind of love life, he managed to keep it private.

Not that a lot of women hadn't tried to catch Daniel's attention. They wrote him love letters, sent gifts and stood outside the gates of his home and stared in, hoping for a glimpse of him. One had even managed to get herself smuggled into his home inside a grocery delivery truck.

Daniel greeted it all with bemusement. He truly didn't understand his own appeal to women.

For the past few minutes, Ford had been laying out the case for Eldon's innocence—the wig fiber, the identity of the woman he'd been with that night, and most importantly, the existence of a witness whose statement, which tended to support the kidnapping theory, had been expunged from the official police report.

Raleigh interjected her legal opinion every so often. Robyn remained utterly silent. Ford had debated whether it was wise to bring her. But if all else failed, he hoped an emotional request might persuade Daniel that he should continue to pour resources into the case.

Robyn was pretty darn compelling.

Daniel appeared to be absorbed in his phone, but Ford wasn't fooled. The man was a master at multitasking. He had heard every word Ford and Raleigh had spoken.

Finally he set his phone aside, placing it in the

raft's cup holder. Ford wondered how many phones he went through because he accidentally dunked them.

Daniel looked up and removed his sunglasses. "It's not enough," he said again.

Ford exchanged a look with Raleigh. Her face didn't change, but she was adept at hiding reactions and feelings. Then he looked at Robyn, and he immediately felt an urge to go to her, put his arms around her. She looked devastated. This would be a good time for that emotional appeal, though he hadn't coached her about this. If it didn't come naturally, Daniel would see through it immediately.

"So, are we calling this one early?" Ford asked.

"I didn't say it was hopeless," Daniel said. "It's just not enough for the governor. One of James Redmond's campaign promises was that he would be tough on crime. He doesn't stay an execution for a convicted child killer without irrefutable physical evidence, or a confession from a person other than the one behind bars."

"So what do you suggest?" Ford asked, relieved that Daniel hadn't said he was pulling the plug. Not that Ford would have given up. On or off the payroll, he would continue working on this case up to the minute of Eldon's execution. He owed it to Robyn after all he'd put her through.

"The witness in Montana," Daniel said. "Roy White. Give him an all-expense-paid trip to Houston. Put him up in a nice hotel. And take him to see Dr. Ellison."

Dr. Ellison was Project Justice's consulting psychologist. She was a master at hypnotic regression. "So you think Roy should undergo hypnosis?"

"Your only chance at this point is if Roy can remember a description of that car in the parking lot, and perhaps a license plate. Even a partial one. That's the only thing that might lead you to an alternate suspect. Governor Redmond *might* stay an execution if he has another suspect to focus on."

Raleigh cleared her throat. "If we hypnotize Mr. White, he'll be useless as a witness later on. You can't put a witness on the stand who has undergone hypnosis—"

"I'm aware of the law, Raleigh." Daniel said this not as a reprimand. He just didn't like wasting time. "I'm more interested in right now. It's the prosecutor's problem if a star witness can't testify."

It would be their problem, too, if Eldon were granted a new trial. But Ford knew better than to argue. Daniel had analyzed the data he'd been provided, made an assessment, and decided on a course of action. It was what he did best. And once Daniel set a course, he stuck to it.

"Put some more pressure on the woman, too," Daniel said.

"Heather?"

"Talk to her husband. He's a man of the cloth—appeal to his humanitarian side. If she's the devoted wife she claims to be, she'll do what he says. Research the man six ways to Sunday, find a weakness and exploit it. Although, I'm not sure anyone will believe her, since Jasperson has never mentioned this woman in the past."

"I'll get on it."

"Good. Will you all stay for lunch? Chef Claude is making crab salad."

Raleigh stood and picked up her briefcase. "I can't, Daniel. I have some papers to file for the Simonetti case. But thank you."

As if by magic, Jillian Baxter, Daniel's assistant, appeared to show Raleigh out.

Robyn stood, too. "I appreciate the invitation, Mr. Logan." It was the first time she'd spoken since being introduced. "But we have five days to find better evidence, and I'm determined not to waste a minute of it." She looked at Ford, daring him to challenge her.

"We have a long to-do list," Ford agreed, closing his notebook and standing. He would be glad to return to air-conditioning. "But I appreciate the offer."

"Rain check, then." Daniel paddled his raft to the shallow end and stood up, rising out of the water almost like a god of the pool. He met them as they headed toward the house, but he addressed Robyn. "I know this is difficult, believe me. Don't give up. You haven't lost yet. I'm not being hard-hearted— you understand that, right? I'll have one chance with the governor. It would be a shame to waste it at this point."

Robyn nodded. "I understand."

"I hear you became the victim of a crime yourself yesterday. You're welcome to stay here, if you like."

"That's very generous of you, Mr. Logan."

"Daniel, please."

"Daniel, then." Robyn nodded, obviously touched by Daniel's gesture. When he chose to reveal his caring side, people had a hard time not responding to it, Robyn included. "But Ford has a perfectly adequate guest room. Since we're working together, it's a little easier if I just stay with him."

A tightness in Ford's chest eased, and he realized with a start that he'd been worried she would choose Daniel over him. And who would blame her? Half the women in the country would give their eyeteeth to stay at Daniel's estate.

A speculative gleam entered Daniel's gaze as he glanced at Ford, and Ford gave a little shrug. Raleigh wasn't the only one who could hide feelings.

CHAPTER TWELVE

"GOOD MORNING. MY NAME IS Ford Hyatt, and I'd like to make an appointment to see Reverend Brinks as soon as possible. I believe he can help with a very sad case, maybe even save a man's life."

Ford crossed his fingers that the church secretary who'd answered the phone wouldn't ask for specifics. He was prepared to lie about his true intent, but he didn't want to.

Funny, lying didn't used to bother him.

"Let me check his schedule. Can I tell him what this is in regards to?"

"It's an extremely private matter."

"I understand. Just a moment."

While Ford waited, he went over the progress on the Jasperson case spread out over his desk.

Two more days had ticked away, with little progress. Receipts arrived from various wig shops, the fruits of Robyn's and Trina's labor. Ford gave these to a Project Justice data analyst, who compiled lists of names and current contact information and compared them with people police mentioned in the original police reports on the kidnapping.

So far nothing had panned out.

Ford had also been checking out the background of Heather's husband. The Reverend Bradley Brinks was as squeaky-clean as they came. The man had led such an exemplary life, it was hard to believe. He paid his bills and his taxes on time, he had no history of drinking or drug use, no ethical complaints filed against him, not even a parking ticket. His congregation loved him; his neighbors loved him. His entire family—parents, siblings—appeared to be scandal free, too.

The reverend's only questionable decision was to marry a girl who lied about her past, but even that was turning out okay so far. Everyone said she was a good wife and mother, a tireless volunteer, kind and generous.

Though Ford had no way to pressure the man, he had to try.

The secretary came back on the line. "The reverend can see you at two this afternoon."

"Thank you. I'll be there."

Ford had assigned Robyn several jobs that would keep her busy. First, she was to convince Roy White to come to Houston, then make all of his travel arrangements. Then she would help the analyst working on the wig receipts.

Frankly, Celeste could have handled these chores. But he wanted Robyn safely busy at the office so he could pursue Reverend Brinks on his own. The interview was likely to get unpleasant, and he didn't want Robyn to see that side of him again.

Then again, seeing him as he really was might serve as a good reminder for her. She'd welcomed sex with him because she had seen a softer side of him. He'd been protective and tender with her injuries, and she suddenly believed that's who he was.

But his inner cop hadn't gone away. He was still the same man who had appalled her by coming down hard on a pregnant witness and a defeated man on death row. He got the job done, but he could be a real bastard sometimes. That hadn't changed.

Robyn viewed him—temporarily—as some kind of hero because he was one of the few people who believed in her cause and was willing to help her. But he wasn't a hero, just a terribly fallible man who was about to become another in a long line of people who had disappointed her.

During his divorce, Kathy had claimed that she'd fallen in love with his potential, not with him. He refused to let the same thing happen with Robyn. She'd had enough heartbreak in her life.

The only thing he could do for her was press forward with the job she'd hired him to do. But he had little hope of success. Daniel's instincts about these things could be depended on. Unless they uncovered something else, something startling and concrete, there would be no stay of execution for Eldon Jasperson.

A couple of hours later he arrived at the church early, and the secretary, who seemed ill at ease, showed him to the reverend's office.

The moment Ford entered, he realized his ruse hadn't worked. The minister was there, all right, but so was his wife. He stood behind his desk in the small, spartan office. Heather looked almost triumphant. Almost. Her unsteady gaze reflected a note of fear, too.

Ford wasn't dead in the water yet. Maybe this could work to his advantage.

"Reverend Brinks. Thank you for seeing me." Ford extended his hand to the minister. Good manners overcame his reticence, and Brinks accepted the handshake, though Ford could tell he didn't want to.

Ford looked at his wife. "Mrs. Brinks. It's nice to see you again."

"I wish I could say the same. My husband knows the circumstances of our first meeting," she said.

Ford could just imagine how that conversation went. What kind of spin had Heather put on the uncomfortable conversation they'd had in her rose-covered living room?

He went on the offensive. "And does your husband know that you are in a position to save a man's life, and you refuse to do so?"

The reverend answered for her. "I find your insinuations regarding my wife not only insulting, but actionable," he said succinctly. "You invaded our home—"

"She let me in."

"You slandered her. I've already contacted my

lawyer. If we ever see you or hear from you again, you can expect legal action. Now leave."

"It's only slander if I tell someone else. Anyway, lawyers don't scare me. But you know what does?" He stopped there. He'd been about to tell the good reverend just how sordid his wife's past really was. But what purpose would it serve?

In his mind's eye he saw Robyn's blue eyes. Honest eyes. Kind eyes. She would be horrified if he degraded Heather in front of her husband. Whatever her past, she was trying to live a good life now.

She obviously had her reasons for not talking up for Eldon.

A disturbing thought occurred to Ford. What if Heather did know something—something that only confirmed Eldon's guilt, rather than exonerating him? If that were the case, in her mind Eldon was exactly where he needed to be, and her involvement wouldn't serve justice at all.

It would just tarnish her reputation, and she wouldn't be the only one to suffer. She had a husband, children.

"What scares you, Mr. Hyatt?" the reverend asked. "Hell?"

"Not anymore. I've been there." He stood up. "I'm sorry to have taken up your time. You won't hear from me again."

As he climbed into his car, he was satisfied with the decision he'd made. Disappointed, sure. But he knew, deep inside, that he'd made the right call not to trash that woman's life out of spite and frustration.

He again thought of Robyn. He was hungry, and he could have stopped for a late lunch, but he didn't. He was in a hurry to get home. To her.

Those feelings directly opposed the decisions he'd made only a few hours ago regarding their lack of a future.

She hadn't pressed him about his afternoon plans, only saying she would wait for him there until he returned. It had been a time since he'd had a woman waiting for him. Even longer since he'd felt good about himself for any reason.

He didn't believe he was capable of wholesale change. But Robyn had brought to the surface whatever good bits were left inside him. Not that he could take seriously any thoughts of a future with Robyn. But maybe, just maybe, he still had something to live for.

ROBYN'S HEAD ACHED AND she was going cross-eyed. For two hours she'd been helping one of Project Justice's analysts, Billy Cantu, decipher information that had been sent from the various wig shops. Who knew this many people in the world bought wigs?

For the last hour, Robyn had been comparing names with a list of hundreds of people connected with the investigation into Justin's disappearance. Maybe the police *hadn't* zeroed in on Eldon too quickly, because they'd sure talked to a lot of people.

Many of those people's names were familiar, but some she'd never heard of. She had no idea what their connections were; she had only the list, not the details of why they were included in the file.

It was after hours by the time Ford returned to the office from his mysterious mission. Most of the staff had left, but several people were still hard at work on their phones or at the computers. She imagined this place never really slept.

Her heart lifted at the sight of Ford. She told herself it was because she couldn't wait to set aside this loathsome task. But that wasn't it. She was glad to see him.

Her body responded more urgently than ever to him as he strode toward the desk where she was working. Now that she'd had a taste of him, she craved him like a drug.

It was a struggle not to reach out to touch him, a struggle to keep from breaking out in a silly grin. She had it bad for the man, and talk about inconvenient.

"Hi. Long day today, huh?" She kept her expression neutral, her body language guarded. But he was such a well-trained observer, he could probably see through her puny efforts to disguise her feelings.

Nothing she could do about that.

"Very long. Any progress?"

"Billy is going through the last batch of receipts

now. I've been comparing names, but so far, no matches. Only one thing…" She debated about whether to mention it, then decided not to. A false lead would only waste valuable resources. She shook her head. "Nah, nothing."

"What?" He pulled a chair next to her. "You were going to say something. Say it."

"It's silly."

"Let me decide. Come on, spit it out."

"Okay. I keep going back to that name, Bella Orizaba. You said you'd have someone check into it?"

"I did. She's an older lady, lives in Galveston. Apparently she's very ill with her third bout of cancer."

Robyn sagged. "So she probably bought a wig after chemo. Another dead end."

"I think we might have had an Orizaba at our school. Maria or Marissa, maybe. Few years younger. That could explain the sense of familiarity you had."

Robyn tried to picture the student Ford referred to, but nothing came to mind. "That's probably it," she said.

"You don't really think so."

She hesitated. "I told you it was silly."

"I'll do some more checking."

"No, really, Ford, I don't want to waste anyone's time. I shouldn't have said anything."

"It's not a waste of time. You have a feeling. I am a

firm believer in intuition, or gut hunches, or whatever you want to call them. I can give her name to Mitch Delacroix, our tech expert. If this woman has any ties to Green Prairie or Eldon, Mitch will dig them up."

"It seems like such a long shot."

"Everything about this case is a long shot. But it's like a piece of fabric. You pull one thread, then another and another, until finally the whole thing unravels. You just never know which thread is going to do the trick."

"Or if the fabric is some new miracle textile that can't be unraveled."

He shrugged. "There is that."

Robyn began tidying up the desk she'd been using, throwing away her coffee cup and putting her scribbled notes into some kind of order—as if they'd be of any use to anyone.

"Have you had any success today?" She didn't quiz him about where he'd been or what he'd been after. If he wanted her to know, he would tell her, and she knew sometimes his investigations involved privacy issues or sensitive information. Even though she was his client, she wasn't meant to know everything, and she accepted that.

He didn't answer right away, and just when Robyn began to think he wouldn't respond at all, he sighed deeply. "No success with the case. I…I went to see Heather's husband."

Robyn felt herself tense. She'd made no objections when Daniel Logan had told Ford to lean on

Reverend Brinks. Though she didn't feel it would help to further bully Heather, Robyn had gone to Project Justice because they were experts at what they did—the best. She couldn't presume to tell them how to do their job, so she'd tried not to think about it.

"Don't worry, Robyn. If anyone left the meeting feeling a bit humbled, it was me. They were prepared for my arrival. She's one tough cookie, your Heather."

"I don't doubt it, given her background. So, you got nothing?"

"I wouldn't say that."

"You seem almost pleased."

"Not about Heather's lack of cooperation. That still irks me. But something else…"

"What?"

"I can't explain it. Not in any way that would make sense to you. But after leaving that unproductive meeting, I actually felt good about the way I handled it. And I have you to thank."

He was right; she didn't understand. "I wasn't even in the same state."

"You were in my mind the whole time," he argued. "I thought about your compassion, and how you don't judge. I've been a judgmental son of a bitch my whole life. Long before I ever sat on a stupid student tribunal who sat in judgment of a young girl and convicted her with absolutely no evidence. But today, for once, I didn't judge. I just walked away, and it felt incredibly good."

Robyn's head was spinning. Ford had made some kind of breakthrough. And though she didn't fully understand what he was talking about, she was happy for him. He certainly looked like a different man from the one she'd found in a seedy waterfront bar, drowning his sorrows.

"It might not be good," he said thoughtfully, "if I want to keep working this job."

"I thought you didn't want to keep working this job," she pointed out as she shouldered her massively heavy tote bag.

That stopped him. "I did quit, didn't I?"

"So maybe you'll rethink it."

"Maybe."

"You know, you shouldn't base your decision on whether you win with Eldon…or lose. This case had a slim chance of success from the very beginning."

Some of the light went out of him, and she could have kicked herself for dousing his sudden… exuberance.

"I'm glad you understand that. The odds stacked against us, I mean. But I don't want to disappoint you. Too many people have."

He didn't realize it, but he'd already disappointed her. Not because of anything to do with his work; his diligence and keen intelligence had impressed her beyond anything she could have imagined.

No, she was disappointed on a more personal level. She'd been ready to admit that the man she'd despised all these years might be worth a second look, might even be worth forgiving…and loving. But he hadn't really changed. The only difference was, he was on her side instead of against her.

She quickly moved on. "I almost forgot—Roy White will be on a plane tomorrow. He should arrive by noon. I've got a car scheduled to pick him up from the airport and take him to his hotel, then on to Dr. Ellison's office."

Ford smiled, accepting the change of subject. "Good work. I knew the VIP approach would work with him."

"Yeah…he's kind of an egotistical jerk." She slapped her hand over her mouth. "Now who's being judgmental?"

"It's okay, I don't particularly like him, either."

"Could he be a suspect?"

"Possible, I suppose, though nothing about his demeanor suggested that. The cop who interviewed him left the Green Prairie force several years ago. I'm trying to track him down. If we could get him to admit someone ordered him to bury Roy White's interview, it could be extremely helpful."

"I take it no one on the police force so far is willing to admit that."

"The cops won't even talk to me. They say I'm wasting my time and they don't want me to waste theirs. Even Bryan Pizak, my old football buddy, has gone quiet."

"Jerks," she muttered.

"Hungry?"

"Starving. I don't know what's wrong with me. I've been eating enough food for three people, and it doesn't seem enough."

"This work burns calories. How about Italian?"

Robyn hesitated. She wanted to avoid anything that smacked of "date" with Ford. On the other hand, her mouth watered at the thought of baked lasagna and garlic bread. If they relaxed for a short while, ate a hearty dinner, they could work for another few hours tonight.

Hunger won out. "Italian sounds great."

"Dr. Ellison, this is Roy White, the man I was telling you about." Ford introduced his possible witness to the psychologist who would wring the details out of his memory, if they were there.

"And this is Sergeant Ken Glasgow with the Green Prairie Police Department."

The short, tubby and humorless Sergeant Glasgow shook Roy's and Claudia's hands, making no comment. Ford had persuaded the police to send an official representative. An impartial witness needed to hear what Roy had to say. They had only two more days to convince the governor to stay Eldon's execution, and a member of the police force would hold more sway than anyone from Project Justice.

Roy White loved attention. He loved the fact that his boss had given him two days off from work, with pay. He loved the free meals and the fancy hotel, the car and driver.

All of these perks had been provided to soften Roy up, to make him *want* to help. If he provided useful information, his name would be in the news. Although the hypnosis he was about to undergo would preclude his ever testifying in court on this case, he might be interviewed by truTV or CNN.

"Roy, it's so nice to meet you," said Claudia Ellison. She was a tall, cool blonde with a warm smile. She turned that smile onto Glasgow, welcoming him just as effusively.

Roy swelled under the charm but Glasgow remained stiff and somber.

Ford had met Claudia his first day working for Project Justice, when he'd been required to take a battery of tests to ascertain his fitness for the job.

He'd figured he would fail. But apparently he hadn't, because he hadn't been dismissed.

Claudia was one of those therapists who made you want to give the right answers. She was an expert at recovering lost memories through hypnosis. Roy warmed up to her right away, chattering about his plane trip—his first experience with first class—not even realizing Claudia's "small talk" was designed to elicit information she needed to evaluate his sincerity and truthfulness as a witness.

After an initial, low-key interview, Claudia had Roy sit in a comfortable chair, and the session began.

Ford, Robyn and Glasgow stayed in the room, but sat out of Roy's field of vision. So although he knew they were there, he would feel as if he were alone with the pretty psychologist.

Claudia took Roy through a series of questions. It seemed like Roy was merely relaxed, talking easily, his eyes half-closed.

"So tell me what happened the night Justin Jasperson disappeared," Claudia asked in a conversational tone.

"I was working a split shift," Roy said. "So I got into work about nine."

"Was it a busy night?"

"No, pretty quiet."

"Anything unusual occur that night? Besides the child's disappearance, that is."

"No. Just an ordinary night. The dining room closed at eleven, so after that we just did to-go orders. The driver, Jeff, left for his last delivery right before midnight. That's when the Jasperson order came in, for a large pizza."

"Did you know the Jaspersons?"

"No."

"Do you remember what kind of pizza?"

"Half-and-half. One side was pepperoni, the other black olive."

Ford looked at Robyn and gave her a thumbs-up. Roy's story hadn't changed, and he appeared to be recalling even more details.

"Did you take the order?"

"No, Mindy, the night manager did. I made the pizza and put it in the oven, then I took my break."

"And what did you do during your break?"

"I went to the parking lot to smoke. There was an area off to the side, near the Dumpster. We weren't allowed to smoke in front of the restaurant."

"What kind of cigarettes did you smoke?"

"I had a joint in my pocket." He no longer seemed bothered by admitting to drug use; Ford had assured him the statute of limitations had long since passed. "I lit that and took a couple of hits. Just a little something to make work bearable. Then I saw a car pull into the parking lot, so I put out the joint and lit a Marlboro."

"What kind of car?"

"Jag. Silver. I remember thinking how I was gonna have a car like that someday."

"Did you see who was driving?"

"I saw Eldon Jasperson get out. I mean, I didn't know him then, but I know who it was now. After all the publicity."

"How did he seem?"

"Seem?"

"How did he act? Was he calm, or agitated?"

"He locked the door with a remote. Then he went right inside. Walking kind of fast but not running."

"Then what happened?"

"I was thinking about that car, you know, imagining what it would be like to drive it—the kind of shit kids think about all the time. Then another car pulled into the parking lot and parked right next to the Jag. I thought that was kind of strange, because the parking lot was empty. The second car could have picked any space."

Ford glanced over at the detective. He sat impassively, not even taking notes, the bastard. Of course, Glasgow didn't want it known that the police had blown their investigation into the biggest crime in Green Prairie history, but at some point he had to drop that agenda and pay attention to the facts.

"What kind of car was it?" Claudia asked.

There was a long pause, and Ford held his breath. Robyn reached over and took his hand in a tense grip. He wondered if she even realized she'd done it.

"It was small. Silver. A Toyota Camry or something similar. Those cars are everywhere so I didn't pay attention."

"Did you note the license plate?"

Another long pause. "PCA," he said matter-of-factly. "Those were the first three letters. I don't know about the rest."

Ford had to control the urge to leap out of his chair and put his fist in the air. This was huge! With a partial license plate, along with the color and a possible make and model, he could track this car down.

He looked over at Robyn, expecting to see her smiling and excited. Instead, she looked stricken, and her face was a deathly white.

"What's wrong?" he whispered. "Are you sick?"

In answer she stood and quietly left the room.

Ford wanted to follow her, but he needed to stay and listen to the remainder of Roy's session. At least

Glasgow seemed to be paying attention now. He'd taken a small notebook out of his breast pocket and was scribbling something.

The remainder of the interview didn't last long. Roy said that he'd finished his cigarette and returned to work right after the second car drove up. He didn't see who was behind the wheel or any other pertinent details. He recalled boxing up the pizza, and then the uproar a few minutes later when Eldon announced that his child was missing.

As soon as Claudia began the process of bringing Roy back to full consciousness, Ford quietly left the room. He expected to find Robyn in the waiting room, but all of the chairs there were empty. Claudia's receptionist was on the phone.

Ford walked out into the hallway, his worry for Robyn ratcheting up a notch. He sank with relief when he spotted her coming out of the ladies' room, mopping her face with a paper towel. She looked shaky, but at least some color had returned to her face.

"Are you okay?" he demanded. "What happened back there?"

"I'm sorry…I had to leave, I thought I was going to be sick."

"Was it something you ate?" he asked, bewildered. People reacted to good news in all different ways, but they usually didn't throw up.

She blinked at him owlishly. "I don't think you understand."

"I understand that Roy White just gave us a huge lead. We stand a very good chance of tracking down that second car."

"You don't have to track it down. Eight years ago, I was driving a silver Honda Accord—very similar to a Toyota Camry. The license plate was PCA 227."

CHAPTER THIRTEEN

ROBYN SAW THE EXACT MOMENT Ford realized the implications of what she was saying. At first he was confused, as if he hadn't heard her right. Then he shook his head, as if that would negate the facts she'd just told him.

Finally he looked her straight in the eye. "You're telling me Roy White just implicated you in the kidnapping and murder of your own son."

She nodded. A few times in her life, she'd been frightened, but not like this. In the span of a few seconds, she'd watched her future, her very life, drain into nothingness.

What she needed more than anything was for Ford to fold her into his arms and tell her this was some kind of terrible mistake, that Roy was mistaken or lying and Ford would straighten everything out by lunchtime.

But he didn't. His bewilderment turned to anger. His face hardened into something Robyn had never seen before. Then he turned on his heel without a word and strode back down the hall to Claudia's office suite.

Robyn didn't know what to do except follow.

She would be brought into the police for questioning, that was a given. She might even be cuffed and incarcerated.

But all she could think about was that look on Ford's face. He'd been horrified, angry.

At her?

He had already dashed her hopes about any sort of romantic involvement, but she thought she would at least have his friendship, his respect.

Now she felt even that draining away. He was all about law and order, right and wrong, and she was about to become a murder suspect.

Never mind that that Roy White was a lying jerk.

Her mind raced. Why would Roy lie? The answer was easy. Someone paid him to lie. Someone was getting nervous, which meant they were closer to the truth than they knew.

Robyn pulled herself together and made herself follow Ford back into the office. The answer was simple. Ford would interrogate Roy and he would crack; he would admit that he was being paid to falsify testimony, and he would give up the name of the guilty party.

But when she entered the waiting room, the scene that greeted her nearly knocked her to her knees. Roy and Ford were shaking hands and Claudia was beaming. All three of them viewed the hypnosis session as a triumph. They'd gotten the information they wanted.

Did Ford actually *believe* Roy?

How could he? Didn't he know Robyn better than that? She had opened herself up to him so thoroughly; she'd kept no secrets from him, not the most private parts of her life. She had offered up everything for his dissection in the hopes of somehow saving Eldon.

He should be angry, defending her innocence. Because if he didn't, who would?

She could survive the coming ordeal, but only if she held on to hope. Ford was the one who could give her that. At the moment, he wasn't giving her anything. He wouldn't even look at her.

Confused, and afraid she would burst into tears in front of everyone, she slipped out of the room, down the elevator, out of the building, finding herself on a street in the busy West University neighborhood far from anything familiar. She struck out aimlessly down the street, needing the release of a brisk walk. It was as hot as a sauna, but she didn't care.

Ford would wonder where she'd gone, but she didn't intend to stay gone long. She wouldn't make any effort to hide; she merely needed some time alone to gather her dignity together.

When the police came, when the media showed up, when the cameras rolled, she wouldn't let them see the pain.

Like Eldon, she'd be stoical. Because if Ford— the man she wanted so badly to love—did not step forward as her champion, nothing else mattered.

FORD HAD KNOWN THE EXACT moment Robyn came into the waiting room, and the exact moment she'd departed. He'd felt her pain, her confusion, but he hadn't been able to do anything about it. He'd been too busy putting on a show for Roy, pretending he believed the lying son of a bitch, and that he didn't realize his client had just been implicated in a murder.

"I need to talk to the Captain about this," Glasgow was saying. He seemed to be taking the turn of events seriously. Ford wished now that he hadn't involved the police. Because now he was going to have to come clean; otherwise he would be guilty of obstructing justice. It wouldn't take a decent investigator long to arrive at Robyn as their new suspect anyway; a cursory examination of the case file would turn up the kind of car she'd owned at the time of Justin's disappearance, including the license plate.

"Just a minute, Sergeant." Ford pressed some cash into Roy's hand. "Here's some cab fare. That should get you back to your hotel. Your plane leaves tomorrow morning. A car will pick you up at 7:00 a.m. to take you to the airport."

Roy nodded. "Is that all? I mean, I could stay a couple more days if you need me for something."

Glasgow eyed Roy up and down, sizing up his credibility, perhaps. "The police will be in touch."

"I'm really glad I could help."

It was all Ford could do not to wipe up the floor with Roy's smug, insincere face.

Roy walked out, and the detective looked expectantly at Ford. "You had something you wanted to say?"

"The car Roy described. It's Robyn's car. You'll find it in the case file."

Glasgow's jaw dropped. He glanced at the door, then back at Ford. "You shouldn't have let her leave."

"She won't run. You have my word on that." He knew that much about Robyn—she would squarely face any accusations against her.

"We'll need to talk with her," Glasgow said. "Sooner rather than later."

Ford knew what "talk" meant. A stifling interrogation room. Two, maybe three detectives hammering on Robyn for hours at a time.

"Just a minute," Claudia said. "Sergeant, there's something you should know. Roy White was lying."

Glasgow raised his eyebrows. "Was he, now? He sounded pretty sincere to me. And I'm a trained interrogator."

"He was lying," she insisted. "Not about the whole thing, just the description of the car. The body language of truth and lies is an emerging, legitimate field of study, and Roy's session was a textbook case."

"You can't have it both ways," the detective said, rocking back on his heels. "Either your witness was telling the truth, in which case we throw out Eldon Jasperson's conviction and arrest his ex-wife, or your witness is lying, and Eldon Jasperson fries as scheduled. Which will it be?"

Ford wanted to throttle the sneering sergeant, but he forced himself to use logic instead of brute force. "You know it's not that simple."

Glasgow seemed to come to a decision, and for the first time Ford saw a glint of intelligence behind the sergeant's pompous demeanor. "I'll do what I can for Eldon Jasperson. Clearly there are elements to this case that were not explored. But I'll expect you to deliver Robyn Jasperson to our headquarters by 8:00 p.m. tonight. You don't, we'll come looking for her."

With that, he nodded and made his exit.

Claudia looked crushed. "Ford, I'm so sorry I didn't convince him. Maybe if I talked to someone else—"

"Going over Glasgow's head will only make him mad." Anyway, right now, Ford had more urgent business. He had to find Robyn.

She wasn't in the hallway, and when he cracked the bathroom door and called her name, he was greeted with silence.

He didn't like this. Although she refused to believe it, Robyn was still in danger. The real murderer was out there. He had persuaded Roy to lie and implicate Robyn; a person would have to be carrying around an awful lot of hate and anger to do that.

He dialed Robyn's cell phone and was relieved when she answered. "Hello, Ford." Her voice was strained.

"Robyn, where are you?"

"I'm walking around the block. I just had to get away by myself for a few minutes. I know you're probably sorry now that you threw in your lot with me, but don't worry, I'm not skipping town."

"I never—for God's sake, come back to Claudia's office, *now*." He knew she was scared. But she'd held herself together for so long, even on caffeine overload, with no sleep and frayed patience. Now wasn't the time for her to fall apart, and he wouldn't let her.

Doubts? How could she, even for half a second, think that Ford had believed Roy?

Not for the first time, Ford wished he still had the powers of a police department behind him. He could look into phone records and find out who the hell had gotten to Roy White.

When he exited the professional building, he spotted Robyn heading down the sidewalk toward him, looking a bit bedraggled from the heat. As she came close, their eyes met and held for a mere second before she looked away.

"I'm sorry I ran off like that," she said stiffly. "I was afraid I would fall apart in front of Sergeant Serious."

His irritation with her melted. She'd been upset; she'd reacted illogically. He couldn't blame her for that.

She glanced around her, as if she expected a horde of cops to come out of the woodwork and slap on the cuffs. "Where is he, anyway?"

"Off to do some fact-checking."

"So he believed Roy?"

"I'm afraid so. He's asked that you report to the Green Prairie police headquarters by eight o'clock tonight."

Robyn closed her eyes for a moment, seeming to absorb the blow. "What about Eldon?"

Of course, Robyn would worry about someone else's welfare when her own wasn't in the best shape. "Glasgow said he would intervene."

"Do you think he'll succeed? Do you think the governor will listen? There's so little time. Just two days."

"Yes, I think the governor will listen. I can't guarantee he'll act, but he's not an unreasonable man."

Robyn almost smiled. "At least there's that. We did what we set out to do."

Yeah, but at what cost?

"Will they arrest me?" she asked in a small voice.

He wished he could reassure her, but he had to be honest. "I don't know."

"I should stop by home and water my plants, just in case." Her attempt at humor fell flat.

"Whatever happens, we'll deal with it."

"Will you? If I'm charged, will Project Justice take *my* case?"

He opened his mouth, ready to say *of course Project Justice would take her case*. But she was talking about Project Justice, not him personally, and it wasn't his place to say yes or no. It wasn't his decision to make. That was only part of the reason he hesitated, however. He paused, carefully formulating what he wanted to say.

But he was too slow. The light of hope left her eyes. "I guess I can't blame you. The evidence points to me. You'd be crazy to champion me without knowing more. I get that."

She turned and waved her arm in the air at an oncoming taxi.

"You're the one jumping to conclusions." He grasped her arm to stop her from waving, hoping the taxi would drive on. "Look, you can't just run off. Let me at least find you a lawyer. If not Raleigh, then someone just as good." *Handle the immediate crisis first. Then they could step back and develop a strategy.* That was how cops worked—how he worked.

The taxi pulled to the curb and he reluctantly released her. Robyn opened the back door, but she paused and faced him before getting in.

"I don't need a lawyer. I'm innocent."

"You can't possibly be that naive. Innocent or guilty, they'll turn you to mincemeat in that interrogation room."

"You forget, I've been through it before. I'll handle it. But thank you for caring what happens to me."

She climbed into the cab and pulled the door closed.

Hell. He really should have handled that differently.

FIVE MINUTES LATER, AS her taxi became bogged down in city traffic, Robyn felt the shock wearing off and wished she could live over the past few minutes. Ford had offered help. He'd wanted to hook her up with a lawyer. And she'd run away like a frightened child. In her position, she should be embracing any support she could get.

But she couldn't deny she'd wanted more from the man she desperately wanted to love. Maybe Ford didn't believe she was guilty, but he hadn't jumped immediately to her unconditional defense, and that was what hurt.

Robyn took the cab all the way home, to Green Prairie. The fare was exorbitant, but she paid it with a credit card. Running up her credit was the least of her worries. She was more concerned about mundane things; what would happen to her art class? Would they give her a few days to wrap up her affairs, put her things in storage? Or would the apartment manager end up throwing her belongings into the street?

Inside her apartment, she wandered around like a ghost, touching her furniture, her dishes, even her soap.

She didn't kid herself—they were going to arrest her. She had no credible defense against Roy's lies, at least not at the moment, and she would probably spend at least tonight in jail.

There, they wouldn't have fancy soap that smelled of grapefruit.

The memory of Eldon on death row made her shudder. Even if she fought this murder charge with every fiber of her being—which she intended to do—she could still end up locked away forever, or executed.

The two parched plants on her balcony needed water again, so she gave them a drink. It was a meaningless gesture, really—they were already dead from the heat and neglect.

Finally, she drove herself to police headquarters. It was a place she knew well. She parked in the lot, took one last breath of fresh air and headed into the featureless cinder block building.

The desk sergeant looked at her in surprise, and she realized that she knew him. Eight years ago, he'd been at the same job. He was a bit grayer now, a bit stockier, but still recognizable.

"Ms. Jasperson?"

"Yes, that's right. I was told to come here by Sergeant Glasgow."

The sergeant appeared just then, smirking ever so slightly. "I didn't expect to see you so soon," he said, almost pleasantly.

"I want to get this over with as soon as possible."

The sergeant said something under his breath. It sounded like, *Don't get your hopes up,* but she couldn't be sure.

He led her down a long hallway and through a set of locked doors into the bull pen, where the detectives worked. It was a small police force, so major crimes, burglary, fraud and missing persons all worked together.

Every one of the cops looked up when she entered. Robin met their gazes squarely, and one by one they looked away.

Sergeant Glasgow opened the door of an interview room and gestured for her to enter. He followed, soon joined by two other male detectives. Neither was familiar.

"Before we start," she said, pulling out a chair and sitting down before they could choose one for her, "am I under arrest?"

"No, ma'am," the sergeant said. "We're just going to have a friendly chat."

She rolled her eyes. "Cut the crap. I've sat through one of your 'friendly chats' before." It had lasted six hours without a bathroom break. She didn't imagine much had changed since then—except they weren't on a fishing expedition this time. A witness had placed her at the scene of the crime.

They started out friendly enough, going through the usual legal warnings. She agreed to talk without a lawyer present. She knew she could stop the questioning at any time and ask for one; eight years ago, she hadn't known that. The knowledge gave her some small comfort.

They started with the preliminaries—her age, her relationship to Eldon and Justin, where she'd lived at the time of her son's disappearance—all the same questions she'd answered a million times, and would probably answer another million.

Sergeant Glasgow had just started to get to the meat of the interview—what she remembered about the night of Justin's kidnapping—when someone knocked on the door.

The interruption was not appreciated, judging from the looks of consternation on all three of the male officers' faces.

A woman poked her head inside the door. "Ms. Jasperson's attorney is here."

The three detectives looked at her. She shrugged. "I guess Ford Hyatt called someone—he said he was going to."

Everyone went silent as the door opened wider. Robyn hoped to see Raleigh Shinn enter the room. Raleigh, at least, was up to speed on the case, and Robyn respected her thoroughness and intelligence. But the dapper, bald-headed and bespectacled attorney who entered was definitely male.

With a start, Robyn realized she recognized him. He was one of Eldon's appeal attorneys, William Purdy. He hadn't gained Eldon's freedom, but Robyn had liked him anyway. He was smart and knew the law, at least. Ford had chosen well.

But did she want him to make that choice for her? If she accepted Purdy as her lawyer, he wouldn't let her continue with the interview and she wanted to get it over with. But maybe Ford was right; innocent people needed lawyers, even if "lawyering up" antagonized the detectives.

She opened her mouth to agree to the attorney when another person entered the room in a flurry of excitement and perfume.

Trina?

Robyn was happy to see a friendly face, and a little bit relieved that she didn't have to face Ford just yet.

"Robyn, don't you worry about a thing," Trina announced. "Ford hired the best criminal defense lawyer in the county. Please, if you don't mind?" She glared at the detectives.

In turn, the detectives all looked at Robyn. The decision was hers, whether to accept legal help or decline. After a moment's hesitation, she nodded.

"I'll accept Mr. Purdy as my lawyer for now."

Purdy smiled. "Very well. Then my client does not wish to answer any more questions at this time."

"But I want to get this—"

Trina quelled Robyn with a warning look, and Robyn stopped. "All right. But I'd like to make it clear that I don't have anything to hide. As soon as I discuss my *innocence* with my lawyer, you can get on with your questions."

The detectives didn't look happy. But at least they hadn't arrested her. She was free to go…for now.

Purdy and Trina escorted her out of the interrogation room. They made arrangements for Robyn to have a formal sit-down with the lawyer early the next morning, after which they would return to the police station to resume her interview.

Another few hours of freedom. All the tension drained out of Robyn, and her knees wobbled.

"You poor thing," Trina said. "I just could not believe it when I heard what had happened."

"Ford called you?" Lately, keeping Trina in the loop hadn't been a top priority for Ford.

"Um…no, honey, it was in the news report on the radio. In fact, the news vans are outside now."

Robyn briefly considered hiding in the ladies' room and never coming out. Facing the press had been difficult with Ford at her side to protect her. Who would protect her now? Trina?

"Trina, you don't believe I'm guilty, do you?" She needed for *someone* to have faith in her.

"Oh, honey, of course not. I mean, you and I had our differences, but you loved your little boy. Anyone could see that."

"Thank you."

"You look exhausted. My car is parked in back. We can sneak out the back door. I'll take you home and feed you a nice meal. Ford said I shouldn't let you go home alone, that it's not safe."

"So you did talk to Ford?"

"I called him when I heard. I wanted to do something. He'd already taken care of the lawyer, but

he said I should come here and make sure you let
Purdy do his job. And he said I shouldn't leave you
alone."

Given the way she'd fallen apart earlier today, she
didn't blame him.

In truth, Robyn didn't want to spend what might be
her last night of freedom by herself. Granted, Trina
wouldn't be her first choice of companion. But Trina
was who she got, and the woman was going out of
her way to be kind.

"All right," Robyn finally agreed.

One of the cops showed them out the back door.
Moments later, Robyn settled into the passenger
seat of Trina's Escalade, reveling in the energetic
air-conditioning and letting her mind go blank.

It wasn't until Trina turned her car onto Sycamore
Lane that Robyn realized "home" meant the Jasperson mansion—the same house Robyn had shared
with Eldon when they'd been married. She hadn't
been back here since Justin disappeared.

The house looked the same, a colonial red brick
with massive white columns and a circular driveway
with a fountain in the middle. Robyn remembered
how impressed she'd been with this house the first
time she'd seen it, so different from the tiny mobile
home where she'd grown up.

Now it struck her as being a bit much.

The trees had grown. A lump formed in Robyn's
throat when she spied the dogwood tree she and

Eldon had planted when Justin was born. It had been just a tiny stick of a thing. Now it was a mature tree, growing near the corner of the front porch.

On closer inspection, the house seemed a bit bedraggled. The trim needed painting, the lawn had bare patches and the flower gardens were filled with weeds. Maintenance on this property was hugely expensive; maybe Trina didn't have the funds to keep it up.

Trina pulled into the three-car garage and cut the engine. The other two bays were filled with old furniture. Robyn recognized a couple of pieces that she and Eldon had picked out for the living room, and the headboard to their bed.

Well, it was only natural for the new wife to put her stamp on the decorating.

Then she spied Justin's crib, and she almost lost it.

She had to remind herself that, on the advice of friends, relatives and her therapist, Robyn herself had dismantled the room she kept for Justin in her apartment. Life went on.

She followed Trina into the house.

"I bet you haven't had lunch," Trina said. "And here it is almost dinnertime. I've got some cold cuts and French bread and maybe some soup from the deli. Would that be okay?"

"Trina, that would be spectacular. I really appreciate it." On impulse, she opened her arms and hugged Trina. Right now, she needed to connect with someone. Badly.

Trina seemed surprised, but after a moment she softened and returned the hug, patting Robyn on the back. "Oh, honey, you would do the same for me if I was in trouble."

Trina's lush black hair tickled Robyn's nose, and she got a strong whiff of shampoo.

Coconut.

The smell was familiar, and Robyn's body reacted to it by producing a rush of adrenaline that made her want to push Trina away and run. The reaction confused her for a moment, until she realized from where she knew the scent.

The person who'd broken into her apartment and assaulted her had used the same shampoo.

Robyn had told Ford her attacker was too small to be a grown man, and was probably a kid. But now she realized it also could have been a small woman.

"Robyn, is something wrong?"

Robyn had pulled back and, still grasping Trina by the shoulders, was staring at the other woman's face, probably with a look of horror.

"You broke into my apartment," Robyn said before she could consider the wisdom of confronting someone who had assaulted her, and possibly had done much worse.

"Excuse me?"

The pieces fell into place. "It's been you all along. You resented Justin. You were jealous of me, and the hold you thought I had on Eldon because he was the father of my child. So you did something about it."

"Have you completely lost your mind? I would never hurt a child. I was cleared as a suspect. Roy saw a woman with long blond hair in that parking lot, and last time I checked, that didn't fit me."

Robyn felt dizzy with the realization. Trina had just cemented her fate. "Roy never said anything about a woman with long blond hair. But he was supposed to, wasn't he? That's what you coached him to say, when you paid him to make up a story."

"I don't know what you're talking about. I never met this Roy person."

"Then you must have talked to him on the phone. You sent him money." Robyn knew she'd said too much. She had to get out of there, away from Trina before the woman did something terrible out of desperation. Something else terrible.

Or before Robyn herself did something she would regret. She had never felt the urge to kill anyone—except the person who had taken her son away from her.

She turned away and reached into her purse, intending to call someone—the police? No, it would take too long to explain.

Ford. He would believe her. He had to believe her.

She'd scarcely gotten the phone clear of her purse when Trina knocked it out of her hand, and it went skittering across the quarry-tiled kitchen floor.

"Don't you dare!" Trina's eyes narrowed, and her artfully painted mouth twisted into a grimace. "Your precious Ford isn't going to run to your rescue this time. This is between you and me."

CHAPTER FOURTEEN

HER HEART POUNDING, ROBYN judged her chances of lunging toward her phone and getting away with it.

Not good. If Trina were capable of killing a child, she wouldn't hesitate to kill anyone. She was small, but strong from regular workouts.

Robyn held up her hands. "Okay, whoa, whoa, time-out. I got a little carried away and I jumped to conclusions. Let's not make this any worse than it already—"

Trina cut her off with a well-placed elbow to the gut, knocking the breath out of her. "Just shut up, okay? I gotta figure out what to do. Your timing is lousy. Another couple of days and I'd have gotten the hell out of this town. I'm not an idiot, you know. I had a contingency plan. I've been socking money away in the Cayman Islands for years, just in case."

Robyn managed to pull some air into her lungs. "In case someone figured out you'd killed Justin."

"I didn't kill him, you moron."

"What?" Robyn found strength she didn't know she had. In one quick movement, she straightened, grasped Trina by the shoulders and shoved her into the refrigerator. "Then who killed him? You know who did it, and you better tell me right now or so help me I'll—"

"Let go of me!" Trina struggled, but Robyn's fury fueled her muscles. "If you don't get your hands off me this instant, you will *never* know what happened to your son."

Robyn instantly let go and backed up. "Oh, God, Trina, if you have an ounce of humanity in you, tell me what happened to Justin." She sank to her knees, the fight gone out of her. She hadn't let herself think about it in a long time, but now she did; she pictured her baby in an unmarked grave, somewhere in the woods or the desert where no one would ever find him.

"Stop sniveling," Trina said. "Get up."

"I won't call anyone. I'll give you plenty of time to get away. Just tell me where I can find—"

"He's not dead, okay? I may not be a saint, but I wouldn't kill a little kid."

FORD'S GUT CHURNED FROM too much coffee and not enough food. He'd violated his own rule about keeping his tank filled; he'd skipped lunch and was on his way to missing dinner.

But the urgency to do something about Robyn's situation wouldn't let him think about something as trivial as his personal comfort.

On Raleigh's recommendation, he'd hired William Purdy for Robyn, whether she wanted legal counsel or not. Ford hoped a lawyer would get through to Robyn where Ford had failed. Civilians simply didn't understand how common it was for innocent people to confess when they were under tremendous stress.

Ford had wanted to do more. He'd wanted to drive to Green Prairie, to be with Robyn, to personally micromanage the fallout from Roy's explosive lie. But he doubted his presence would be welcome.

So he focused on what he *could* do to help her, from a distance—namely, tearing apart Roy White's statement and his credibility.

Mitch Delacroix, the tech expert at Project Justice, had been put to work hacking Roy's home and cell phone records. It wasn't legal, but if they could find out who he'd been in touch with, they would know who had bribed him.

Ford had briefly considered Roy as a suspect— maybe he'd made up the story about Robyn to cover his own tracks, and he hadn't been bribed at all. But without an accomplice, he would have had no way to make Justin disappear, because he was back at work a mere five minutes after the child went missing.

Either way, he was working with someone.

Ford was doing what he did best—working potential witnesses. Roy had family, friends and associates, and these were easy for him to find. Whenever he got someone on the phone who knew Roy, he asked if Roy had mentioned coming into some money, or if he'd announced plans to make a large purchase like a new car or a TV.

He quickly found out that Roy was not generally liked or respected, even by his own family, and most of the people Ford talked to were eager to dish.

Roy had told many of them about his trip to Houston, and the fact that his witness statement was going to save a man from execution and maybe catch a murderer. But none could remember anything about money—until Ford located one particular coworker.

"Oh, yeah," the man said. "He's been wanting to buy a Harley for, like, five years, and just yesterday he was on the phone talking to a dealer about it. He sounded pretty serious about buying it."

Ford was encouraged. At a motorcycle dealership, there might be a paper trail to follow—or at least some notes made regarding the phone call. He was about to ask the coworker for more details when something caught his eye. He looked up to see Celeste standing in the doorway with a young woman in tow. He stopped talking midsentence when he recognized the woman.

"I'll have to call you back," he told his contact on the phone. Then he hung up and stood. "Heather."

"She insisted on seeing you right away," Celeste said. "When she mentioned that it was about the Jasperson case I knew you would want to see her."

"Of course. Thank you, Celeste."

Celeste stood expectantly in the doorway as Heather entered the office with tentative steps, looking terrified.

"Can I bring you something to eat or drink?" Celeste asked in an überpolite voice that was a total put-on. She was just nosy, and she was trying to find a way to learn more about their visitor.

"Some soft drinks, please, and maybe a couple of sandwiches," Ford said. "Close the door behind you."

"I don't need anything," Heather objected.

"It's okay, I'll eat what you don't want. Sit down, please. You don't have to be afraid. I give you my word I won't raise my voice or make any more threats. I apologize for the way I treated you before."

Ford came out from behind his desk and indicated Heather should sit in one of the wingback chairs. He took the other one.

"What can I do for you?" He held his breath, afraid that if he spoke too stridently or moved too quickly, she would bolt. Only one thing could have brought Heather Boone to his office—her conscience.

Heather worried at a button on her shirt. "I talked to Brad. I told him everything. He's such a good man. I don't deserve him." She broke down into tears.

Wordlessly, Ford found a box of tissues in a drawer and handed it to her. He thought ahead to what he would do if she confessed. She wouldn't be able to leave the building. Celeste would be on her guard. One phone call from Ford and she would lock the front door, then tackle and cuff Heather herself if necessary. She might look harmless—until you crossed her.

While Heather brought herself under control, Ford
pulled a small digital recorder from a drawer, set it on
the desk between them and hit the record button.

Heather looked at it, but didn't object. After another minute or so, she was able to talk again. "The
night Justin disappeared, I was with Eldon. I was at
his house. He…he went for pizza. We were going to
have it delivered but then it was about two minutes
after midnight and the restaurant didn't deliver after
midnight—" she paused to gulp in some air "—but
I was really hungry and there was nothing in the
house so Eldon said he would go pick it up, but then
Justin woke up and he was crying and I didn't know
what to do because I was only eighteen and I'd never
been around kids before, so Eldon said he would take
Justin with him because he always fell asleep in the
car."

Ford didn't know whether to be relieved or disappointed. On the one hand, Heather's statement supported Eldon's story in every detail. If Justin was
alive at shortly after midnight, there is no way Eldon
had time to kill him and dispose of the body, then
show up to pick up the pizza ten minutes later.

But Heather's statement didn't in any way exoner-
ate Robyn.

"I know I should have said something then. But
I figured if Eldon needed my help, he would have
told the police about me. And I was so scared to get
involved, scared someone would think I'd done it. I

was the girl from the wrong side of the tracks and I'd been in trouble with the law before.

"So I just left. I got out of town. I knew it was over with Eldon, and there was nothing else in Green Prairie for me. I didn't look back. I never watched the news or read a newspaper because I didn't want to know. I turned myself into someone else. But the past has a way of coming back."

"Yes, it does," Ford agreed. "I know how hard this must have been for you, but would you be willing to make a formal statement to police?"

"Wait, I'm not done. There's something else."

Ford went still. "Go ahead."

"I stood on the front porch as Eldon got in his car and drove away. The gate opened and he pulled out into the street. He turned right onto Sycamore, and just after that I saw another set of headlights come on. A car was parked on the street, just outside the gate. It started up and took off after Eldon's car. I remember thinking it was odd, because in that neighborhood no one parked in the street."

"Did you see the other car?" Ford's heart pounded so loud in his ears, he was afraid he wouldn't hear Heather's answer.

"I saw it just for a second as it drove past the gate. It was fancy—European, I think. And red."

Red, not silver. Ford was so relieved, he almost missed the rest of what Heather was saying.

"Oh, and it made a chugging noise. Like a truck. A…um, one of those different kind of engines—"

"Diesel?"

"Yes, that's it."

Something clicked in Ford's memory. "Excuse me, Heather, I have to check something." The case file was on his desk, and he paged through it frantically. Yes, there it was. At the time of the kidnapping, someone very close to the case drove a red Mercedes sedan. A diesel.

Trina Jasperson.

He grabbed the receiver from the phone on his desk and dialed Robyn's cell number. He got her voice mail. That in itself wasn't immediately alarming; if she were still answering questions at the police station, her phone would be turned off.

"Does that mean something?" Heather asked. "The red car?"

He'd forgotten she was there. The recorder was still running, and he clicked it off. "You've been very helpful. Thank you for having the courage to come here today."

He practically dragged her to her feet and out the door. They nearly ran over Celeste, who was coming their way with a tray of sandwiches and drinks.

Celeste eyed them both disapprovingly. "Leaving so soon?"

"Celeste, see Mrs. Brinks out. Get her a cab, if she needs one. Heather, I'll be in touch."

"O-okay."

As he headed down the hall to the stairs—the

elevator was too slow—he was already dialing Trina's number on his cell phone.

Trina didn't answer, either.

Ford had a bad feeling in his gut. Something was wrong, very wrong, and he'd learned to always trust his gut.

ROBYN FELT DIZZY AND, for a moment, she thought she would pass out. Justin was alive?

"Stand up!" Trina ordered her. "You do what I tell you, and I won't hurt you. I'll give you all the information you need to find your kid."

Robyn's head spun as she scrambled to her feet. Justin, alive. After all these years, was it possible? Her mind teemed with possibilities, most of them horrifying. Had he been sold into slavery overseas? Such things did happen. If her child was alive, what kind of life had he led? One of constant brutality and fear? Would she be able to find him?

Trina grabbed Robyn's shoulders and swiveled her around roughly until she faced a double louvered door. It led to a large broom closet. "Go through there."

Robyn's legs were so watery that she had a hard time walking. But the promise of learning Justin's fate was a powerful motivator. She put one foot in front of the other, reached the door and shoved it open.

"Well, go on. Go inside."

Should she blindly follow Trina's instructions?

Every instinct told her to fight back. But what if Trina made good her threat and never revealed what she'd done to Justin?

Robyn stepped inside the closet. Trina reached past her and grabbed a broom, then quickly closed the doors and shoved the broom through the door handles, effectively locking Robyn inside. There were no windows, no other way out.

Panic rose inside her chest, but Robyn tamped it down. "Tell me now, please. Please."

"You've ruined everything. You know that, don't you?" Trina said in a huff. "I knew it was only a matter of days or even hours before someone figured it out, but I thought it would be those wig receipts that did me in. That's why I was in your apartment. You said you'd had a batch of receipts mailed to your house by mistake—from the wig shop I bought from. But I couldn't find them. Is that how you knew?"

Keep her talking. Robyn could almost hear Ford's voice encouraging her. So long as Trina kept talking, Robyn would stay alive, and she might discover the fate of her child.

"I figured it out because of your shampoo," Robyn said. "I recognized the smell, from when we wrestled on the floor at my apartment."

"Just now? Oh, that is rich. I'm a hairstylist, convicted by shampoo." She paused. "But you haven't told anyone else. Your precious Ford is probably running around, trying to prove your innocence."

"Trina, about Justin—"

"I'll get to it." Robyn could hear Trina moving around the kitchen, going through drawers and cupboards. "I never planned to take Justin. I knew Eldon was having an affair, but I wanted proof. I was going to take pictures, so I'd have plenty of ammunition when I took him to the cleaners in divorce court. So I signed up for the convention in Corpus Christi, and I waited until late that night and I drove back home."

"But you had an alibi," Robyn argued. "Your roommate said you were at the bar until late, and then you both went to bed and you were there all night."

"My roommate was seventy-two years old, half-senile and deaf as a post. Ten o'clock was late to her. She was snoring within five minutes of going to bed. I left and came back and she never knew the difference."

"Okay. So you drove home to check on Eldon—"

"She was right there. Standing on *my* front porch wearing *my* Dolce & Gabbana robe. I parked on the street, watching the house and waiting for a chance to—I don't know. I don't know what I planned to do. I had a gun in my purse, maybe I was gonna shoot him or something. I was so angry, *so* angry."

Robyn longed to tell Trina that she knew exactly how she felt. Exactly. But she didn't want to antagonize the woman who held her life in her hands.

"It surprised me when he got in the car with Justin and they left. I was curious, so I followed him. He pulled into the pizza place parking lot, and I drove past and turned around. I saw him getting out. I saw that he left Justin in the car, alone, and that's when the idea came to me."

Robyn closed her eyes, steeling herself against whatever Trina told her.

"I would take Justin. I would scare the hell out of Eldon and teach him a lesson. I had a couple of wigs in the car, because we had a wig-styling seminar the next day, so I put on the blond one."

"To implicate me," Robyn added.

"You? I wasn't even thinking of you. The other wig was dark, and I wanted something that didn't look like me, in case of witnesses. But I didn't see anyone around."

"You didn't see Roy White standing near the Dumpster smoking?"

"Don't get me started on Roy, the greedy bastard. If he was ever there, he was gone by the time I pulled up. I had the code to Eldon's car. I unlocked it, took the kid—he was drowsy, didn't complain. I got back in my car and drove away, thinking I was pretty clever. Thinking how frantic Eldon would be.

"I was going to bring him back ten, maybe fifteen minutes later. But when I drove past again, the cops were already there. Flashing red lights everywhere, and I realized I was going to get in trouble. I'd kidnapped a child that wasn't mine. I got scared. I drove to my mother's house.

"We planned to just leave him somewhere, you know, some place where he would be found. But then

Mama had another idea. She knew of a couple in Mexico, some second cousins of hers, I think. They wanted children and couldn't have them, and they were trying to adopt but there was so much red tape and expense."

Robyn's knees buckled, and she sank to the floor. "You sent my child to Mexico."

"It was so simple, and I thought it would solve all my problems. No more stepkid taking up all my husband's time, attention and money. No more ex-wife to deal with—God, I hated you. Such a saintly, devoted mother. Eldon worshipped you."

Despite the obvious error in Trina's thinking, Robyn didn't argue. She swiped at the tears leaking from her eyes. "What happened to my baby?"

"I told you. He went to live with a couple in Nuevo Laredo, Mexico. That's all I know."

"What's their name?" Robyn asked. "The couple?"

Trina hesitated. "I don't know. But why would you want to find him after all these years? You'll just ruin his life."

Was Trina crazy? "I want my baby."

Another long pause. "Valdez," Trina finally said. *Valdez, in Nuevo Laredo.* There were probably a zillion Valdezes in that city. Robyn would check them out one by one if she had to. When she got away…if she got away…she would find her baby.

"Thank you, Trina."

The other woman sighed. "Yeah, well, I guess I owe you that much." She actually sounded regretful.

And Robyn almost felt sorry for her. Things hadn't gone as she'd planned. She'd probably never realized that Eldon would be the most likely suspect. She'd managed to get rid of Heather, and the crisis had drawn her and Eldon closer. But the life as Mrs. Eldon Jasperson, respected member of society, never materialized. Instead she became the wife of a purported child murderer.

"So what now?" Robyn asked. "Are you going to kill me?"

"Don't be so melodramatic. I haven't killed anyone yet, and I don't plan to start with you. By the time someone finds you here, I'll be long gone and you won't ever find me."

Robyn took a moment to absorb that news, to revel in the fact that she was going to live, and maybe see her baby again, if Trina had told the truth.

If Trina got away…that would be bad, but not the worst thing that could happen. "What about your mother?" Robyn asked, trying to kill time. Sooner or later, Ford would come looking for her. She had to believe that. "Won't she be in trouble, too? Are you taking her with you?

"She's dying. Cancer. What's the worst they can do to her?"

Dying—cancer. "Your mother is Bella Orizaba." Eldon must have mentioned his mother-in-law's name to Robyn at some point.

The doorbell rang.

Ford. It has to be Ford. "Aren't you going to get that?"

The chimes sounded twice more, then a strident voice yelled through the door. "Open up, Trina! I know you're in there."

The police? Then Robyn realized she knew that voice.

Trina swore viciously. "What's he doing here?"

"He came to collect," Robyn concluded. "Better let him in. I don't think he's going away."

The doorbell sounded again, three times, then the banging resumed. "I'm coming in, Trina, one way or another. And you won't call the police, because how would you explain my being here?"

"Robyn, seriously," Trina said frantically. It sounded like she was shoving something inside a drawer. "Don't say anything." Then she went to answer the door.

"Are you crazy?" Trina shrieked. "Why did you come here?"

"You said you'd pay me as soon as I said my piece to the police. Well, I did you proud. That half a license plate did the trick. The cops were falling all over themselves to thank me—"

"You have to go! What if someone sees your car in my driveway?"

It didn't sound like Roy White was leaving. In fact, it sounded like he was coming toward the kitchen.

"You want me to go? Pay me what you promised."

Robyn debated her chances of gaining rescue by

calling for help, then kept her mouth shut. She had disliked and mistrusted Roy White from the moment she'd laid eyes on him. He was a user, an opportunist. Robyn would take her chances with Trina, who had at least showed some signs of remorse.

"Half now," Trina said firmly. "Half when you repeat your story to the cops."

"How about all of it now, or I break your arm?"

Robyn stifled a gasp. If he hurt Trina, Robyn would be helpless to stop it. If she screamed or tried to stop him, he would likely turn on her.

"Come on, Roy, there's no need for this." Trina's voice was high, panicked. "I have lots of money. I'm going to Mexico. Beautiful beaches, nonstop piña coladas. You could come with me."

While Trina wheedled, Robyn got down on her hands and knees. She could see Trina's high-heeled sandals, and Roy's work boots. He had her backed up against the kitchen counter.

"You're gonna live down there?" Roy asked curiously.

Robyn saw something else; her cell phone on the floor, where it had fallen, forgotten. It was only a couple of feet away.

"Money goes three times as far down there," Trina was saying. "I got a beach house all picked out."

Robyn grabbed an economy-size box of dishwasher detergent and tore it open with her hands, her fear giving her strength. The powder spilled out all over her. She tore the box lengthwise down two corners, then put it on the floor and flattened it with her feet until she had one long piece of cardboard. She felt like she was making a terrific amount of noise, but Trina and Roy were so wrapped up in their own drama, they didn't seem to notice.

On her hands and knees, Robyn slid the cardboard out under the door. She could just reach the phone. She couldn't pull it toward her, but she could nudge it sideways.

She pushed it all the way to the left, where it ran into the bottom of a set of cabinets. Now she could rake it toward her.

There, she almost had it. Just a couple more inches—

Her phone rang.

Roy halted midsentence. "What the hell?"

Robyn slid the phone those last two desperate inches, and it was in her hand. She grabbed it—Ford was calling her. She pressed the talk button.

"Ford, thank God, I'm locked in Trina's broom closet. She did it, Ford. She took Justin—" Robyn realized she was talking to dead air. Her phone had already rolled over to voice mail.

Roy rattled the broom stuck through the handles of the louvered door. "Oh, my God," Roy said on a laugh, "you've got the blonde locked in here." He pulled the broom loose from the door handles.

CHAPTER FIFTEEN

ROBYN FELT LIKE AN ANIMAL in a cage. She grabbed the first weapon she could find, a bottle of glass cleaner. And when Roy shoved the door open, she sprayed him full in the face. The assault slowed him down only a moment as he sputtered in surprise. Robyn took that moment to grab a mop and jab him hard in the stomach with it.

Trina screamed, and in the confusion Robyn had just enough time to speed-dial Ford back.

"Robyn? Thank God. Listen—"

"Help me, Ford. I'm at Trina's and I—" Roy's fist connected with her jaw. She dropped the phone and fell back into the brooms, which clattered to the floor all around her. Her vision clouded with sparkles of pain and she sank to the floor.

"Leave her, Roy," Trina said harshly. "It's too late, we have to get out of here."

"And leave her behind to blab everything to the cops?"

"We still have time to get away. The border's not that far. I have people there who can help me— help us."

"No one knows my part in this yet. You can go to Mexico if you want, but I'll take the cash, thanks."

Robyn was perfectly aware of what that meant for her. Roy didn't intend for her to tell the cops anything.

"Please, come with me. I—I need you," Trina said unconvincingly. "Oh, God, Roy, don't."

Robyn's vision cleared, and the next thing she saw was a gun in Roy's hand.

FORD WAS DOING NINETY-FIVE down the highway. He hadn't bought himself a Crown Vic for nothing.

His attempt to rouse the Green Prairie Police had been met with an indifferent, "We'll send a patrol around." Without hard evidence that Robyn was in peril, they wouldn't take some ex-cop's "gut instinct" seriously, especially not his.

Not when his efforts were going to make their department look incompetent at best, and at worst, willfully, criminally guilty of withholding evidence.

So he'd taken matters into his own hands. He had rallied the Project Justice troops. Anybody in the building with a law enforcement background had dropped what they were doing and piled into his car—even Celeste, Lord help him. They hadn't questioned him. He'd said Robyn was in trouble, and they'd dropped what they were doing to help.

That kind of loyalty was hard to find. He'd made mistakes, and he hadn't exactly gone out of his way to bond with his fellow investigators, but they were behind him anyway.

Later, he would have to rethink his decision to resign from Project Justice. Right now, though, he had to save Robyn's life.

He'd been only a few miles from Green Prairie when her urgent and frighteningly brief phone call had come through; that was when he'd floored it.

"Can't this heap go any faster?" Celeste demanded from the backseat.

"Got it floored," Ford replied.

Beside him, Joe Kinkaid had a white-knuckle grip on the door handle, but he didn't suggest that Ford slow down. In the backseat, Billy Cantu and Mitch Delacroix also had nothing to say about his excessive speed. The gravity of Robyn's situation weighed heavily on all of them, and the only conversation involved what strategy they would use when they arrived at their destination.

The only strategy Ford intended to use was to break down the door and storm the place.

"You've picked up an escort," Joe reported calmly.

Sure enough, Ford saw flashing lights in his rearview mirror. He wouldn't bother stopping; the more cops he could drag to the scene, the better.

"Next exit," Billy announced. He had mapped their destination on his cell phone. Though Ford knew where the Jasperson house was—he'd seen the location on a map in the case file—he'd never actually been there.

He took the exit and slammed on his brakes as he approached a light.

"Right turn."

A car was in his way, waiting for the light. Ford went over the curb, narrowly skirting a telephone pole and a lamppost, quickly checking for cross traffic before clunking down onto the street.

"Quarter mile, then a left turn."

He was mere blocks from the house. *Hold on, Robyn.* God, he loved her.

Loved? Why hadn't he seen that before? Why hadn't he told her? It might have made a difference.

In those few tense moments as he pulled into the driveway through the open gate, he saw with crystal clarity how much he loved her, and how wrong it had been to hold back. He had feared disappointing her or being somehow "wrong" for her, but his seeming indifference had wounded her deeply.

Give me another chance. He would make it right.

Before his car had even come to a stop, the doors opened and his team poured out. Billy and Joe headed around to the back of the house; they would look for a way in, and no one trying to escape would get away.

Ford planned to make entry at the front, no warning; they might draw fire, if anyone was armed, but they had on Kevlar vests, at least. Full SWAT gear would have been better, but they worked with what they could grab on the fly.

The police car on their tail pulled in and the officer jumped out, weapon drawn.

"Police! Stand down!" His voice squeaked. He looked scared to death.

"Oh, pipe down," Celeste said as she tightened her own vest. In her hand she had a gun almost bigger than she was.

"Hostage situation," Ford announced. "You can arrest me when it's over."

The front door was huge, imposing and looked like solid wood. Celeste sized it up, then, with the determination of a charging rhinoceros, ran at it full tilt and hit it with her shoulder. She bounced right off.

"Celeste, don't hurt yourself."

"Oh, please," she grumbled as she tried again to get through, executing a pretty good karate kick with her booted foot. The wood actually cracked.

Ford thought the tall windows flanking the door looked more promising. He was about to pick up a potted fern and use it to bash through the glass, when Celeste halted him with a tug to his sleeve.

"Look here, Ford." She opened the door in the usual way. "It wasn't locked."

"We're inside," Ford said into the walkie-talkie attached to his vest, the channel left open so he could talk hands-free. The cop, apparently not knowing what else to do, followed them in.

"Police!" he announced. "Drop your weapons and—"

Trina screamed, and Ford followed the sound of her voice, using what little cover he had—a half wall, a dining room chair.

When he looked into the kitchen, he saw Trina backed up against the counter, her hands already in the air. Roy White—what the hell?—stood in the middle of the kitchen, a gun in his hand but looking confused and indecisive.

"Put your weapon on the ground," Ford said, aiming for Roy's head. "You have to the count of three. One, two—"

With a look of resignation, Roy stooped and set his gun on the floor. He raised his hands.

"Get on the floor!" Ford shouted as he stormed the room. Celeste was on him like a feral cat and had him cuffed almost faster than Ford could blink.

"Nice," the surprised cop murmured from behind them.

"That's a skill forty years in Vice will get you," Celeste said.

Ford focused on Trina. Knowing what she'd done, what she had put Robyn through, made it tempting to shoot her on the spot. "You, too. On the floor. Where is Robyn?"

Trina didn't answer as she shakily lowered herself to her hands and knees, but she didn't have to, because Ford spotted Robyn. She stood in the doorway of a closet, covered in white powder. The side of her face was red, as if she'd taken a blow, but otherwise she looked…there were no words to describe it. She was a goddess. His salvation.

By then, Billy and Joe had joined them. Seeing that his team and the confused Green Prairie cop had Roy and Trina well in hand, Ford went to Robyn and wrapped her in his arms. "Are you okay?"

"I think so." She returned his hug fully and didn't seem to want to let go.

"What happened to your face?"

She pulled back enough that she could rub her jaw gingerly and look into Ford's eyes. "Roy hit me."

The fury that washed over Ford almost had him turning and kicking the son of a bitch in the ribs. But he would have to let go of Robyn to do that, and he wasn't willing to.

"It's okay. I sprayed glass cleaner in his eyes and put a broomstick into his gut, so I guess he was kinda mad."

"That's my girl."

"Oh, Ford, Trina kidnapped Justin. All this time—"

"I know, I know. Heather Boone cracked. She told me enough that I figured it out. But Robyn, you have to know one thing. I never in a million years thought you were guilty of anything. But I didn't have the authority to—"

He stopped, sighed. No, that wasn't the real reason. Officially, Project Justice couldn't accept a case unless Daniel gave the okay. But in practice, if any of his lead investigators felt strongly in favor of a case, Daniel would agree to take it on.

"I hesitated," he said, "only because I was afraid of failing you. I couldn't bear the thought of trying to help you and screwing it up somehow. I didn't want your life in my hands."

"I can't think of anyone I would trust more with my life."

Her trust was a gift, one he didn't deserve. "I was wrong to hesitate. I would go to the ends of the earth for you. Even if I failed you, and I still might, I'm not afraid. I'm with you a hundred percent, no matter what."

She hugged him again. "And I'm with you. Ford, there's something else." Her eyes sparkled with joy and hope like he'd never seen before. "Justin is alive. Trina said her mother took him to Mexico."

"Okay," the cop interrupted. "If you're done with this little lovefest, want to tell me what's going on? And why I shouldn't drag you straight to jail? You were doing ninety-five."

Robyn's eyes widened in alarm. "Ford!"

"Did you want saving or not?" He hugged her again and whispered in her ear, "I love you, you know."

FORD INSISTED ROBYN GO to the hospital and have her swollen jaw x-rayed. Robyn obeyed, if only to remove herself from the chaos of being the victim in the middle of a crime scene.

An hour later, as she sat shivering in an over-air-conditioned treatment room at the Green Prairie Medical Center with an ice pack numbing her throbbing face, she finally had a few minutes of peace and quiet to savor the news that Justin, her baby, was alive. She held this new reality close to her heart, keeping it safe.

She also recalled what Ford had said.

His faith in her felt warm and comforting; nestled inside her, his love was a cherished, unexpected gift. She hadn't had the chance to tell him of her own feelings, but she felt sure he knew. She loved him. That stupid student council court from high school didn't matter anymore.

She wished he had come here with her, but the scene at Trina's house had been insanely confused. The cops arriving in droves on the scene didn't know whether to give Ford a medal or cuff him.

Someone tapped on the door to her room, then entered before she could say anything. She relaxed only slightly when she saw it was the young doctor who had sent her to X-ray.

"Good news, there's no fracture," he said with way too much cheer. "Do you want a scrip for pain?"

She shook her head. "It's not that bad." And she had a feeling she would need a clear head for the next few hours.

"Then you're set to go home."

Hah. The police wouldn't let her go home for some time. Then there was Eldon. Despite Daniel Logan's personal intervention, she'd heard nothing about the governor calling a halt to the execution, and the hours were ticking away.

Surely the governor would stay the execution now—if he could be contacted and made to understand all that had just happened. But however that washed out, Robyn had to tell Eldon that Justin was alive.

The young officer who had driven her to the hospital was still waiting when she got her discharge papers. She had a million questions she wanted to ask; she wanted to know where Ford was. But the cop was apparently under orders to tell her nothing, because she couldn't get a shred of information out of him as he drove her back to the police station.

The debriefing was every bit as grueling as she'd expected. Rather than an interrogation room, she and three detectives—the same three who had questioned her earlier—were in someone's office and she had a more comfortable chair. But other than that small concession, she was treated little better than when she'd been a suspect.

Robyn was patient as long as she could be, painstakingly going over the events, but finally she'd had enough.

"Look, I know this is complicated, but is anyone talking to the governor? Because if someone doesn't do something soon, a man is going to be executed for a crime he didn't commit. And what about my son? Trina said he's alive. Is anyone doing anything—"

"We're following up," one of the detectives answered with an infuriating lack of interest.

"And Ford? You didn't do something stupid like arrest him, did you?"

The detectives all looked at each other. They reminded her disturbingly of Larry, Curly and Moe.

"That's it." She got to her feet. "Arrest me for something, or let me go."

They didn't seem happy about it, but they allowed her to leave. She wasn't sure exactly where she would go—her purse, car keys and cell phone had all been left behind at Trina's house, part of the crime scene. She would call Project Justice, she decided. Someone there would come to her aid.

As it turned out, she didn't have to call anyone. Ford was waiting for her in the police building lobby, holding a shopping bag.

Without hesitation, she rushed into his waiting arms. "I thought I'd be bailing you out of jail."

"I thought so, too. But they got so busy with Trina confessing all over the place and Roy loudly proclaiming his innocence, they kind of forgot about me." He gently stroked her swollen jaw. "You look like a lopsided chipmunk. Shouldn't you still be at the hospital?"

"I'm fine. Nothing's broken." But as she eased herself out of Ford's embrace, she wobbled on her feet, and Ford kept one arm around her waist to steady her as they exited the building. It was dark out.

She checked her watch. "How soon can you get

me in to see Eldon? I have to see him and let him know that Justin—"

"You'll have lots of time for that."

As the meaning of Ford's words sank in, Robyn wanted to weep with relief.

"I just heard from Daniel," Ford went on to explain. "The governor stayed Eldon's execution. Obviously, there will have to be a new investigation, but I feel certain he'll be pardoned and released."

"Oh…oh, that's great!" Now her eyes filled with tears. She no longer loved Eldon, but the relief of knowing he wouldn't die for a crime he didn't commit was like a tidal wave washing over her.

Her legs simply wouldn't hold her up any longer. She sank to the edge of a concrete flower bed and sat down.

"There's something else I have to tell you," Ford said. "It's about Justin."

Robyn braced herself for the worst. "Was Trina lying?" Over the past few hours, Robyn had tried not to get her hopes up. Trina might have been manipulating her, holding out the promise of Justin's return simply to keep Robyn cooperative.

"I went to her mother's house. I wanted to get there before she found out about Trina's arrest, before she started destroying evidence. But there was little chance of that. She's sick. Dying, actually. She's in hospice care."

"Were you able to talk to her?"

Ford nodded. "Her conscience was getting to

her. She wanted to tell someone, before she died. She placed Justin with a cousin of hers in Mexico, a woman and her husband who desperately wanted children. They've been raising him as their own. Trina's mother says the boy is happy and healthy."

It was too much. Robyn broke down and heaved huge, heavy sobs as Ford rubbed her shoulders and murmured vague words of comfort.

"Can we find him?" she finally managed when she could speak again. "Will I ever see him again?"

"Yes, to both questions." Then she discovered what the shopping bag was all about. It was filled with photos of Justin and letters from the cousin. There in the heat of the summer night, in the blue light of a buzzing streetlamp, Robyn looked at all of the pictures of her son. There were twelve in all. She watched Justin grow before her eyes from the chubby toddler she remembered to a strapping boy of ten.

"He looks happy," she said, not quite sure how this made her feel. "He's smiling in every picture. He has friends and look—he plays soccer. Oh, and look at this one. He has a dog. Can I keep these? I want to read the letters."

"I'll have to turn them in to the police as evidence," Ford said. "But we can make copies before I do that."

She gently, reverently, placed the photos back into the shopping bag. Then she threw her arms around Ford's neck and kissed him with every ounce of passion she had in her body, and then some.

"I love you so much. Thank you, thank you for giving my son back to me. Maybe you're not ready to have me in your life full-time. Maybe you're not ready to take on my complications. But I just want you to know—"

"Whoa. Who said I wasn't ready to take you on full-time?"

"Well, it's just that—I'm sure you didn't expect to suddenly have a child thrust into your life."

"I will welcome you and any child of yours into my life with no reservations. I love you, Robyn, with everything that's in me. If you hadn't come into my life, I don't know what would have become of me. I might still be sitting on that bar stool at McGoo's."

She couldn't deny that he'd changed since that day. She'd watched him come alive as his love for the work he did overcame his fear that he couldn't always do it perfectly.

He had brought changes into her life, too. If not for loving him, she might still be stuck inside herself, too sad and guilty to allow herself any enjoyment in her life.

"He'll need a tire swing," Robyn said, completely out of context. "I always wanted one when I was a kid."

But Ford was right there with her. "Not just a swing, but a backyard. A neighborhood with trees and other kids to play with. A house. We'll buy a house."

They sat for over an hour in that unromantic

parking lot, spinning dreams about their future. Neither of them had said a word about marriage, but Robyn hoped Ford would be ready for that, someday.

CHAPTER SIXTEEN

FINALLY, THE HOT SUMMER had broken. It was early September, and a cool rain had fallen all morning. Now, though, the sun broke through. Ford used an old towel from the trunk of his car to dry off a wooden bench at the Green Prairie City Park.

Robyn sat down, then slid her arms out of her raincoat.

Ford sat beside her and took her hand, intertwining their fingers. "Nervous?"

"More nervous than I was the first time I held him in the hospital. I was so scared back then, worried if I would be capable of caring for such a tiny, helpless person. I worried that he might reject me.

"That must sound silly. Of course a newborn is going to love his mother. But a ten-year-old boy who doesn't even *remember* his mother..."

"He will love you," Ford said. "The decisions you've made regarding Justin—"

"Arturo," Robyn corrected him. "His name is Arturo now. We have to remember that."

"Anyway, most women would not have been as generous. What you've done is extraordinary."

"All I had to do was think what was best for him, and the decision was made," she said.

Justin—Arturo—knew he was adopted. For the past two months, investigators, lawyers and social workers had been looking into the matter of the boy's "adoption" by a family in Nuevo Laredo.

Although there had never been any formal papers drawn up, his adopted parents, Pedro and Estella Valdez, believed he had been placed willingly in their care by his relatives. Trina's mother had told them the parents died in a car accident, and that's what they'd told Arturo.

From all accounts, they had been devoted and loving parents who had given their adopted son a happy, secure life. Arturo was healthy and thriving.

Suddenly discovering his biological parents were alive had surely been a shock. And though it was her right, Robyn wasn't about to rip the child away from the only home he'd known, his loving parents and friends and pets, and thrust him into a world of strangers in a foreign country.

She wasn't willing to completely give him up, however.

A white Buick pulled into the parking lot, and Robyn tensed. "That's them."

"I'll take a walk," Ford said. "Give you some time alone."

"No." She refused to let go of his hand. "You're part of this. I want you here."

He smiled warmly at her. "Then I'll stay."

The passenger door opened and the boy climbed out. Robyn's heart pushed into her throat. Oh, God. It was really him. Justin was alive. It wasn't a dream.

She waved to him and stood up. He saw her and waved back, tentatively. She resisted the urge to run to him and hug him—she was afraid she would never let him go. Her arms had been so empty for so long.

He was taller than she thought, leaner. He'd probably had a growth spurt recently and lost some baby fat. He was a young man, not a baby.

Robyn clamped a hand over her mouth and willed herself not to cry. That would only make him uncomfortable.

Arturo looked at the social worker, who had just gotten out from behind the wheel of the car. She smiled and nodded. Then he walked toward Robyn, eagerly, it seemed to her. He carried something in a plastic bread bag.

"Hello, I am Arturo. It is nice to meet you," he said in his best schoolbook English.

"*Me llama* Robyn. It's wonderful to see you again," she returned in his language. Her Spanish was pretty good. Being a teacher in South Texas, she'd had to learn.

"We speak English?" Arturo asked. "I want to learn better."

Robyn smiled. "Yes, we can speak English. This is Ford."

"Your husband?"

She touched the diamond ring on her left hand. "We're getting married in two months. What do you have in the bag?"

"Oh—bread," he said a little self-consciously. "You said we meet in a park. Parks have birds."

Robyn had read the letters from his adoptive mother over and over, wanting to learn as much as possible about her child. One thing she had learned was that he loved animals. He had two dogs, a cat, a goat and a one-legged pigeon he had rescued.

She looked around now and didn't see any pigeons or sparrows. "We can walk to the lake," she suggested. "The ducks will like your bread."

He seemed pleased by that suggestion.

"So you are my real mother?" he asked as they walked slowly toward the small lake at the center of the park. The social worker followed at a polite distance.

"I'm your birth mother," she said. "I had you until you were two-and-a-half years old. But then you were taken from me."

"You think I was *muerto*. Um, dead. I think you are dead, also."

"I bet you were surprised to find out I wasn't."

"I was happy," he said simply. They'd reached the edge of the lake, where a few white ducks and a pair of mallards were feeding. The birds came right over when they saw that Arturo had bread. He threw them a handful of crumbles, and they all made a dive for the bits of food, splashing and creating quite a ruckus.

Arturo laughed and threw them some more.

"I was happy, too." She wanted to tell him how she grieved for the years they'd been apart, the years of his growing up that she had missed. But she wasn't sure his English or her Spanish would be adequate.

"Mama—my other mama—cried."

"I'm sure she was scared. She didn't know about me. She was afraid I would take you away. But, Arturo, I won't do that. I mean, if you were unhappy, of course I would... You're not unhappy, are you?"

He shook his head.

"I am so grateful to your mama and papa for raising you, for giving you a happy home. But I do want to see you. I want us to get to know each other. I need you to be part of my life."

The bread was gone, and the ducks paddled away. Arturo balled up the plastic bag and tucked it into the pocket of his crisp, new blue jeans. "I want that, too. I always feel a little different, yes? Everybody has black hair but me."

Arturo had thick, sandy-brown hair. Straight like hers, but closer to Eldon's color. "Was that bad, being different?" she asked cautiously as her fierce maternal instincts roared to life.

"Not really. It made me special in a way. But still, different. I always want to know—there were no pictures."

They all found another bench and sank down,

facing the placid lake. "Now you don't need pictures," she said, studying him, drinking in the sight of him. "You look a little like your—like Eldon."

"My real father. What should I call you?"

Robyn had dreamed of Justin calling her Mama, or Mom. But that would have to be his choice. "What would you like to call me?"

"I thought maybe Prima," he suggested tentatively. "Because you were my first...my first mother."

Robyn was touched. "I would like that."

"Do I have any brothers and sisters?" he asked suddenly.

Robyn and Ford shared a look, and Ford smiled and turned away. "No," Robyn said. "You were my only."

"But you might...I mean, when you get married." Arturo seemed embarrassed.

"Yes," Robyn said. "That could happen. Would you like a little brother or sister?"

"Oh, yes," he said enthusiastically.

"We'll get right on that," Ford said with a grin, and Robyn had to resist the urge to elbow him. When Ford had proposed the week before, they had talked about children. Robyn wanted more. She'd been raised as an only, and she'd wanted a house full of kids. Ford liked the idea, too. But they had agreed it would be too much, that it might complicate the relationship they wanted to build with Arturo.

But maybe it would make things even better.

"So, I know we just met," Robyn said, "and you

don't have to decide right away, but do you think you might want to come stay with us sometimes? Over Christmas vacation, or during the summer?"

"Would Mama and Papa let me?"

"If you want to." The lawyers and the social workers had already talked to Pedro and Estella. Everyone had agreed this would be the best, most fair way to handle the custody issue, at least for now. During the school year, Arturo would remain in Mexico, where he had friends and a history. But he would spend summers and vacations in Texas with Robyn and Ford.

Eldon would have liberal visitation rights. He had been the first to point out that he was hardly ready to be a father. He had to regain his health first, then figure out what to do with his life.

"Then I like to come here and visit. You have pets?"

"I thought that was something we could do together. We can go to the shelter and you can find a dog or cat for us."

He seemed satisfied. "It will be good, then. I will have two houses." He laughed nervously. "People will think I am very rich, with two houses."

"You'll have lots of family, too. Many, many people who love you very much." She couldn't help herself; she had to hug him. She slid one arm around his narrow shoulders and pressed her other hand against his face, pulling him against her shoulder.

To her surprise, he not only welcomed the hug but

also returned it with exuberance, throwing his arms around her neck and clinging to her fiercely.

"I love you, *mi niño*," she whispered, knowing it was too much too soon.

"Te amo, mi madre," he whispered back.

That was when she knew he felt it, too, the connection between them that time and distance hadn't severed.

When they pulled apart, she saw that Ford was watching with a dopey expression on his face. He dabbed at one eye with a finger, then looked away.

"So," Robyn said briskly. "Are you hungry?"

"Yes, very hungry!"

"There's a really good Mexican restaurant down the street…." She trailed off when she saw that Arturo was giving her a look children used exclusively for a parent who had just said something really stupid.

Even Ford shook his head.

"Right, dumb idea," Robyn said. She'd been thinking he might like something that reminded him of home. "How about Denny's? They have hamburgers and fries and really good chocolate shakes."

Arturo nodded. "I like chocolate."

The awkwardness eased. Arturo chattered about school and friends, alternating between English and Spanish, and Robyn shared a few stories about when he was a baby, which he clearly enjoyed. And for the first time in a very long time, the tension left Robyn's chest, and she knew everything was going to work out.

She would finally have her family. Maybe it wasn't a storybook family. There would be complications and disagreements. If she had another baby—and she had to confess, she was already in love with the idea of Ford as a baby-daddy—that would add more craziness into the mix.

They had so much to learn from each other, about each other. But so long as there was love—and there would be lots of love, that was about the only thing she was sure of—they'd be okay.

Ford took her hand under the table and squeezed it.

"Thank you," she said softly, at the exact moment he said the very same thing.

* * * * *

Follow the PROJECT JUSTICE *team as they try to right another wrong in Kara Lennox's next book,*
NOTHING BUT THE TRUTH.
Someone is out to ruin attorney Raleigh Shinn.
Is the culprit the handsome reporter
Griffin Benedict, looking for a juicy story,
or are there more sinister forces in play?
Be sure to find out in March 2011!

COMING NEXT MONTH

Available March 8, 2011

#1692 BONE DEEP
Count on a Cop
Janice Kay Johnson

#1693 TWO AGAINST THE ODDS
Summerside Stories
Joan Kilby

#1694 THE PAST BETWEEN US
Mama Jo's Boys
Kimberly Van Meter

#1695 NOTHING BUT THE TRUTH
Project Justice
Kara Lennox

#1696 FOR BABY AND ME
9 Months Later
Margaret Watson

#1697 WITH A LITTLE HELP
Make Me a Match
Valerie Parv

REQUEST YOUR
FREE BOOKS!

2 FREE NOVELS
PLUS
2 FREE GIFTS!

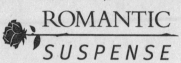

Silhouette®

ROMANTIC
SUSPENSE

Sparked by Danger, Fueled by Passion.

YES! Please send me 2 FREE Silhouette® Romantic Suspense novels and my 2 FREE gifts (gifts are worth about $10). After receiving them, if I don't wish to receive any more books, I can return the shipping statement marked "cancel." If I don't cancel, I will receive 4 brand-new novels every month and be billed just $4.24 per book in the U.S. or $4.99 per book in Canada. That's a saving of at least 15% off the cover price! It's quite a bargain! Shipping and handling is just 50¢ per book in the U.S. and 75¢ per book in Canada.* I understand that accepting the 2 free books and gifts places me under no obligation to buy anything. I can always return a shipment and cancel at any time. Even if I never buy another book, the two free books and gifts are mine to keep forever.

240/340 SDN FC95

Name	(PLEASE PRINT)
Address	Apt. #
City	State/Prov.	Zip/Postal Code
Signature (if under 18, a parent or guardian must sign)	

Mail to the **Reader Service:**

IN U.S.A.: P.O. Box 1867, Buffalo, NY 14240-1867
IN CANADA: P.O. Box 609, Fort Erie, Ontario L2A 5X3

Not valid for current subscribers to Silhouette Romantic Suspense books.

Want to try two free books from another line?
Call 1-800-873-8635 or visit www.ReaderService.com.

* Terms and prices subject to change without notice. Prices do not include applicable taxes. Sales tax applicable in N.Y. Canadian residents will be charged applicable taxes. Offer not valid in Quebec. This offer is limited to one order per household. All orders subject to credit approval. Credit or debit balances in a customer's account(s) may be offset by any other outstanding balance owed by or to the customer. Please allow 4 to 6 weeks for delivery. Offer available while quantities last.

Your Privacy—The Reader Service is committed to protecting your privacy. Our Privacy Policy is available online at www.ReaderService.com or upon request from the Reader Service.

We make a portion of our mailing list available to reputable third parties that offer products we believe may interest you. If you prefer that we not exchange your name with third parties, or if you wish to clarify or modify your communication preferences, please visit us at www.ReaderService.com/consumerschoice or write to us at Reader Service Preference Service, P.O. Box 9062, Buffalo, NY 14269. Include your complete name and address.

SRS11

USA TODAY *bestselling author Lynne Graham*
is back with a thrilling new trilogy
SECRETLY PREGNANT, CONVENIENTLY WED

Three heroines must marry alpha males to keep
their dreams...but Alejandro, Angelo and Cesario
are not about to be tamed!

Book 1—JEMIMA'S SECRET
Available March 2011 from Harlequin Presents®.

JEMIMA yanked open a drawer in the sideboard to find
Alfie's birth certificate. Her son was her husband's child.
It was a question of telling the truth whether she liked it or
not. She extended the certificate to Alejandro.

"This has to be nonsense," Alejandro asserted.

"Well, if you can find some other way of explaining how
I managed to give birth by that date and Alfie not be yours,
I'd like to hear it," Jemima challenged.

Alejandro glanced up, golden eyes bright as blades and
as dangerous. "All this proves is that you must still have
been pregnant when you walked out on our marriage. It
does not automatically follow that the child is mine."

"'I know it doesn't suit you to hear this news now and I
really didn't want to tell you. But I can't lie to you about it.
Someday Alfie may want to look you up and get acquainted."

"If what you have just told me is the truth, if that little
boy does prove to be mine, it was vindictive and extremely
selfish of you to leave me in ignorance!"

Jemima paled. "When I left you, I had no idea that I was
still pregnant."

"Two years is a long period of time, yet you made no
attempt to inform me that I might be a father. I will want
DNA tests to confirm your claim before I make any deci-

sion about what I want to do."

"Do as you like," she told him curtly. "*I* know who Alfie's father is and there has never been any doubt of his identity."

"I will make arrangements for the tests to be carried out and I will see you again when the result is available," Alejandro drawled with lashings of dark Spanish masculine reserve.

"I'll contact a solicitor and start the divorce," Jemima proffered in turn.

Alejandro's eyes narrowed in a piercing scrutiny that made her uncomfortable. "It would be foolish to do anything before we have that DNA result."

"I disagree," Jemima flashed back. "I should have applied for a divorce the minute I left you!"

Alejandro quirked an ebony brow. "And why didn't you?"

Jemima dealt him a fulminating glance but said nothing, merely moving past him to open her front door in a blunt invitation for him to leave.

"I'll be in touch," he delivered on the doorstep.

What is Alejandro's next move? Perhaps rekindling their marriage is the only solution! But will Jemima agree?

Find out in Lynne Graham's
exciting new romance
JEMIMA'S SECRET

Available March 2011
from Harlequin Presents®.

Start your Best Body today with these top 3 nutrition tips!

1. **SHOP THE PERIMETER OF THE GROCERY STORE:** The good stuff—fruits, veggies, lean proteins and dairy—always line the outer edges of the store. When you veer into the center aisles, you enter the temptation zone, where the unhealthy foods live.

2. **WATCH PORTION SIZES:** Most portion sizes in restaurants are nearly twice the size of a true serving and at home, it's easy to "clean your plate." Use these easy serving guidelines:
   - Protein: the palm of your hand
   - Grains or Fruit: a cup of your hand
   - Veggies: the palm of two open hands

3. **USE THE RAINBOW RULE FOR PRODUCE:** Your produce drawers should be filled with every color of fruits and vegetables. The greater the variety, the more vitamins and other nutrients you add to your diet.

Find these and many more helpful tips in

YOUR BEST BODY NOW

by

TOSCA RENO

WITH STACY BAKER

Bestselling Author of
THE EAT-CLEAN DIET

Available wherever books are sold!

PRESENTING...THE SEVENTH ANNUAL
MORE THAN WORDS™ ANTHOLOGY

Five bestselling authors
Five real-life heroines

This year's Harlequin More Than Words award recipients have changed lives, one good deed at a time. To celebrate these real-life heroines, some of Harlequin's most acclaimed authors have honored the winners by writing stories inspired by these dedicated women. Within the pages of *More Than Words Volume 7*, you will find novellas written by Carly Phillips, Donna Hill and Jill Shalvis—and online at www.HarlequinMoreThanWords.com you can also access stories by Pamela Morsi and Meryl Sawyer.

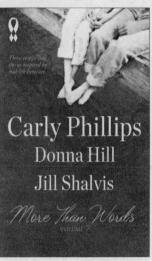

Coming soon in print and online!

Visit
www.HarlequinMoreThanWords.com
to access your FREE ebooks and to nominate
a real-life heroine in your community.

Proceeds from the sale of this book will be
reinvested in Harlequin's charitable initiatives.

MTWV7763CS

Top author
Janice Kay Johnson

brings readers a riveting new romance
with

Bone Deep

Kathryn Riley is the prime suspect in
the case of her husband's disappearance
four years ago—that is, until someone tries
to make her disappear...forever. Now
handsome police chief Grant Haller must
stop suspecting Kathryn and instead begin
to protect her. But can Grant put aside the
growing feelings for Kathryn long enough
to catch the real criminal?

Find out in March.

Available wherever
books are sold.

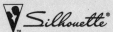

ROMANTIC SUSPENSE

Sparked by Danger, Fueled by Passion.

CARLA CASSIDY

Special Agent's Surrender

There's a killer on the loose in Black Rock,
and former FBI agent Jacob Grayson isn't about
to let Layla West become the next victim.

While she's hiding at the family ranch under Jacob's
protection, the desire between them burns hot.
But when the investigation turns personal,
their love and Layla's life are put on the line,
and the stakes have never been higher.

A brand-new tale of the

Available in March wherever books are sold!

Visit Silhouette Books at www.eHarlequin.com

SRS27718